Transactions with the Fallen

Other Books by Michael Elcock

A Perfectly Beautiful Place (Oolichan Books, 2004)
Writing on Stone (Oolichan Books, 2006)
The Gate: A Story of Love and War (Ooolichan Books, 2012)
*Eyes of Rain and Ragged Dreams:
Coming of Age in Edinburgh* (Muckle Knock, 2017)
(also available as an audiobook)

Visit the author online at
www.michaelelcock.com

Transactions with the Fallen

Michael Elcock

Rock's Mills Press
Rock's Mills, Ontario • Oakville, Ontario
2024

Published by
Rock's Mills Press
www.rocksmillspress.com

Copyright © 2024 by Michael Elcock.
All rights reserved, including the right to reproduce this book or portions thereof in any form whatsoever. For information, please contact the publisher.

This is a work of fiction. Names, characters, businesses, places, events, locales, and incidents are either the products of the author's imagination or used in a fictitious manner. Any resemblance to actual persons, living or dead, or actual events is purely coincidental.

For retail, library and bulk orders, please contact the publisher at customer.service@rocksmillspress.com.

For Xan

December 27: Before you went to Newfoundland

I watched you fall asleep tonight. Your hair was tumbled on the pillow; your wee face beautiful in the soft lamp light. The night wind was blowing, swaying the little shell mobile outside your window and rustling the trees. Far off across the water a light was shining. The light was still, reflecting on the sea; it was not a boat.

It is hard to tell when sleep takes over. Your breathing barely changed and I watched, feeling the peace of our child. Some nights, sleep comes upon you with little twitches and jerks. Tonight it was difficult to tell when it came, you were so serene. I could have stayed all night, stroking your hair, giving you my love.

I shall miss you when you're gone, and I will go into your empty room and remember this night, remember how it was to sit with you and send you off to your dreams.

You can have my star my little love; take it with you to watch over you, as it has watched over me. It will keep you safe.

and for Fionnlagh, and Rich

> If understanding is impossible, knowing is imperative,
> because what happened could happen again.
> PRIMO LEVI

> And everything became dry at once in the flatness of the plain
> in the stone's despair the eroded power
> in the empty land of sparse weeds and thorns
> where carefree on its way a snake glides by . . .
> GEORGE SEFERIS, *THE LEVANT JOURNALS*

Contents

NIGHT NOISES
The Peanut Seller ... 13
Night Noises ... 17
African Postscript ... 27
Warts ... 29
Kojo and the Robin ... 35
The Doodlebug ... 40
Queenie ... 51
Deux Chevaux ... 75

TRANSACTIONS WITH THE FALLEN
The Piano Player ... 85
Transactions with the Fallen ... 93
Agam Prunt ... 111
Danang ... 126
Cardozo ... 132
Covid-Nineteen ... 134
The Stones of Gleann Meurain ... 140
The Stones: Handing on the Task ... 147
The Stones: The End, and the Beginning ... 156

Acknowledgements and Notes ... 161

Night Noises

There were always drums before the rains. They came up the valley on the morning breeze, drifting along the edge of consciousness like a faint, agreeable scent. The sound carried for miles; steady, rhythmic, haunting. It was folded into the haze of laterite dust, a gentle bass to the calls of cockatiels. It was said that the people of the plains would track a stranger with the drums; that they could send a message across the country in an hour.

* * *

You would imagine things in the stillness of the night, when there was no wind to slap the acacia, the only sound the buzz of a cricket. You knew it was perilous out there. You'd been told not to play at the back of the house because a snake had a nest there; to stay out of the flood ditch because danger lay under the fallen leaves at its foot. When night fell it was as if every creature was in the darkness, holding its breath.

M.E.

The Peanut Seller

Peanut vines grew across the ground in the back garden, twisted and tangled. The boy dragged his feet through the vines, stooping now and then to pick off a shell, which he would crack before popping the sweet nuts in his mouth.

The cook called to him from the kitchen window. "It is time to go to the river now. Will you come with me?"

The boy went inside, and watched the cook gather up the dirty pots and pans and put them in a canvas bag.

"You must wear your hat because of the sun," the cook said to the boy.

The cook closed the front gate. A young man was walking down the laterite road towards them. He was barefoot, wearing ragged blue shorts and a grey shirt. Around his neck he had a length of string which was knotted through a hole in a big piece of flat-beaten tin that hung at his chest. It caught the sun and flashed as he walked.

"*Ina kwana*," said Emille, then he remembered that the boy beside him did not know the Hausa language. "Good morning."

The young man returned the greeting with a wave of his hand, and walked on.

"Why is he wearing that thing round his neck?" said the boy, turning to look back at the young man.

"The disk? It is to offer a point of light to the cobra," Emille said. "His house is beyond the village, and he has to cross a meadow to reach it. If there is a cobra in the grass and it spits it will spit at the disk and not at his eyes. He will be safe. He will not be blinded by the venom."

The boy took this in even though he thought it a strange thing.

They walked on towards the river, the cook and the boy, hand in hand. When they reached the river they climbed down to the waterside, and the boy watched as the cook scooped up a handful of black river silt and scoured it around one of the pots.

"Why do you do that?" he asked. He was only five.

"The dirt cleans the pot," Emille said. "It scours it out better than a brush." He was cook but his job was also to look after the boy, and to give him some teaching. He spoke four languages, two European and two native, including his own Hausa language. He rinsed the pot in the water and lifted it to show the boy. The metal shone in the bright sun.

"Are there fishes in the river?" the boy asked.

"Some," said Emille. "Not as many as there used to be. When people are poor and there are no jobs there are more fishermen, less fish."

The boy took this in. He was full of questions. Every question he asked gave rise to another. He glanced up at the sun. It was almost at its height, almost finished climbing. This time he only said, "We should go now. My father said he would take me with him at noon, to the airport."

Emille scoured the last pot, rinsed it, and held it up to the sun. "They are nice and clean. Ready for cooking supper tonight," he said.

He stuffed the pots back into the canvas bag, and hoisted the bag over his shoulder. He rose to his feet and held out his hand. The boy took it and they climbed the bank to the road. It was only a short walk to the house.

On the road they came upon a young woman. She was making her way to the river, a large clay carafe balanced on her head. Emille stopped and greeted her. Because he was with the boy, he spoke in English. The young woman replied in English, bowing her head ever so slightly so as not to unbalance the carafe. "Good morning Emille," she said. She looked at the boy. "And good morning to you too, young sir."

"Good morning," the boy said. "Is it heavy?"

"The calabash? No, it's not heavy. It is made of fine clay from Tasmaske." She smiled, and the boy thought she was beautiful. "Besides, there is nothing in it. After I go to the river and fill it with water, then it will be heavy."

"Will you carry it back the same way? On your head?"

"Yes, I shall," the young woman said, "and it will be as heavy then as you are." Her eyes went to his feet, and slowly back up to his face. She smiled. "Perhaps not quite as heavy as you."

Emille said a few words to the young woman in their Hausa language. The boy did not speak Hausa, and he did not understand what was said. But he noticed that the young woman's face darkened, and that her eyelashes trembled. Then he saw her face light in a smile and her gaze full on Emille's gaze. She turned away, and Emille and the boy walked on.

After a minute Emille said, "Did you like Atikah?"

The boy was watching a bird. It was a large brown bird with light-coloured flight feathers on its underside. It was hovering, high above some bush a hundred yards away. "Atikah?"

"Yes. The young woman we just met."

"She liked you," the boy said. "What did you say to her?"

"I told her I would ask her father if we could marry."

"The bird. What is it?" He did not want to talk about Emille getting married.

Emille followed the boy's pointing hand. "Snake Eagle. They eat Boomslang and Puff Adder."

The boy knew the Boomslang and the Puff Adder were the most dangerous of snakes. He had been told by his mother not to play on the west side of the house because a Puff Adder had a nest behind one of the stilts there. He had had a bad dream about the baby Puff Adders coming up through the floor into his bedroom.

"They must get bitten. Don't they die?"

"No," said Emille. The boy still had hold of his hand. They walked on towards the house. Then, "Perhaps you know Atikah's father. He sells peanuts by the pyramids."

"Why?" said the boy.

"Why does he sell peanuts?"

"Why don't they die? The Snake Eagles?"

"I don't know," Emille said. "I think it's because they have especially thick skin on their legs. Perhaps if the snake can deliver a bite to their bodies it is different. But when the eagle takes it in its talons the snake can't reach up that far."

The boy knew the sacks of peanuts that rose in great pyramids to the sky. There were three pyramids; thousands and thousands of sacks, filled with peanuts. They came to the pyramids in the afternoon when he went with his father to the airport. His father stopped at the third pyramid as he always did, and gave the old man who sat on a box at its foot a clean white handkerchief. The man unwrapped the handkerchief and took out a coin and dropped it in a tin, and filled the handkerchief with peanuts as he always did, and handed it to the boy. They were the finest peanuts the boy had ever tasted. They were not sweet like the fresh peanuts on the vines in the back garden. The old man's peanuts had been toasted, and sprinkled with salt; a pinch only of salt, but fresh-roasted the old man's peanuts were finer than anything the boy had ever tasted before.

The old man was generous and kind. He always gave the boy more peanuts than his father had paid for. The old man had told him two days before that he would grow up and marry his beautiful daughter Atikah.

Night Noises

There was no electricity where they lived. No streetlights, no night light in the house, only kerosene lamps in the kitchen and sitting room. His mother put the boy to bed each night when the sun went down. She lit a wick in a cork that floated in a jar of palm oil and water. They said prayers, "Gentle Jesus meek and mild, look upon a little child…" and then she would give him a kiss and go to join the boy's father in the sitting room. When the oil was used up the light went out. By then he was usually asleep. This was how bedtime was normally conducted.

Once in a while his mother would forgo the prayer and tell the boy a story. One night she tucked him in bed and opened a small book. She read from it. "The kingdom of heaven is like a treasure hidden in a field, which a man found and covered up. Then in his joy he goes and sells all that he has and buys that field."

"It's a very short story," the boy said.

"It's called a parable," his mother said. "It's a story that teaches us something important. The story is more about what you take from it."

"What does it mean?" the boy said.

"It means that being selfish or greedy are bad things."

The boy was puzzled. "I don't understand," he said.

His mother thought for a moment. "The man wanted to keep the treasure for himself. He didn't want anyone else to have it; he didn't want to share it."

"But he found it," the boy said. "It was his."

"The field belonged to someone else," said his mother. "Just because the man found something in it didn't mean he could take it."

The boy thought about this. He was wide awake now. "If the treasure wasn't locked up, it would be easy for someone to take it. How would they know they couldn't just take it?"

"I suppose it depends whether the person who owned the field knew the treasure was there," said his mother. "Perhaps it was gold, or buried pirate's treasure, and the man who found it wanted to keep it for himself. He calculated that if he sold everything he had he could buy the field, and the treasure would be his."

"Would he have to dig up the whole field to get the treasure?" the boy said.

"You mean, if he'd only found some of it? Enough to know there was much more?"

"Yes."

"Then I suppose he would," said his mother. "It would depend on how greedy he was if he just found some of it and believed there was lots more buried in the field."

"But then he wouldn't have a field any more, would he."

"No, I suppose not." She leaned forward and stroked his hair, pushing it back from his forehead. "That might be the true cost of acquiring the field."

The boy looked up at her. "No field left," he said.

The wick was puttering in the jar. The oil had almost gone.

"It's something for you to think about," said his mother. "Something to send you into the arms of Morpheus." She tucked the bedsheet over his shoulders, and under his chin.

"Morpheus?" The word made him sleepy all by itself.

"Morpheus is the God of Sleep. He will give you dreams. Good dreams." She kissed him on the forehead, pulled down the mosquito net and quietly left the room.

The boy had been talking at the front gate that day to a Taureg man, a Berber from the desert far to the north of where they lived in Kaduna. The Taureg had told him that he had come south in search of work; that the oasis where his people had always taken water had been stolen from them by a rich company that wanted the water so they could put it in bottles and sell it and make money. Because there was no longer water, the Taureg man had said, his people were having to change their lives. The Taureg man appeared in his dreams that night; a tall man with bandages wrapped round his head.

"What if the treasure was something like water and it had been stolen?" the boy said to his mother at breakfast.

His mother thought for a moment, and understood that the question came from the parable. "The riches that nature gives us belong to everyone. Water belongs to everyone. Everyone needs things like water and air in order to live; and earth to grow things. You cannot steal them and sell them. It is immoral."

"But what if you just found it hidden in jars or bottles?"

"Well, you would know it belonged to someone else."

"How would I know?"

"It's not natural that something like that would be in bottles or jars. Someone must have put them there for a reason."

Sometimes, in the dark of the night, a strange noise would wake the boy. One night when the wick-candle had gone out and everything was black dark, he was woken up by a fearful noise. It frightened him and made his heart beat fast. He called for his mother. His father came to him instead. He was wearing his pajamas. "What's the matter son?" he said. But the noise had stopped.

"An awful noise woke me up. It was something roaring. It frightened me."

His father lifted a corner of the mosquito net and sat on the bed. He held the boy's hand and listened. "I can't hear anything," he said after a minute.

"It's stopped. Some of the time it was like screaming."

"It must have been a leopard," his father said. "They make that sort of noise. It will be in the jungle. It might be looking for a mate. It won't come into the house."

The boy wasn't sure whether to believe his father. He hadn't seen a leopard where they lived. Besides, the forest was miles away, beyond the airfield where his father worked.

When it rained, the rain drummed on the roof and woke him up. The house had a metal roof, corrugated so the rain would run off to gutters where it could be funnelled by pipes into barrels. The March rains brought water, fresh water, sweeter than the water from the river, which they had to boil before they could drink it.

Some nights, rustling noises would come from the ceiling above his bed and wake him up and frighten him. He knew there was an attic between the ceiling of his bedroom and the metal roof. He didn't know what was in the attic; what might be making the noises that came from there. When he asked his mother she told him it was the wind; that it was causing the metal roof to shift and scrape against the roof joists. She said it was nothing to be afraid of. He trusted his mother so he believed her.

One night the strangest of sounds woke him up. It was after midnight, and very dark. It was a rhythmic, crunching noise, and it went on and on and he didn't like it. It was coming from the other side of his bedroom door. He was afraid to get up and open the door to see what it was. Then he heard a noise of running water coming from the kitchen, and the sound of a burner on the gas stove lighting with a pop.

He heard his father's voice. "Is that pot boiling yet?"

"Yes." It was his mother's voice.

"It won't be enough. We'll need more. Put on another pot."

The boy got out of bed and put on his slippers. Carefully he opened his bedroom door. In the hallway was a black river, flowing from the front door, past the kitchen to the back door. It was making a loud, champing, grinding noise.

"What is it, father?" he called, and his voice was unsteady.

"It's all right," said his father from the kitchen. "It's army ants. They migrate when the rains come, and they eat everything in their path. Come and look at what they've done to the carpet. They won't bother you if you stay out of their way."

But the boy didn't come out. He stayed in the doorway, and smelled paraffin. His mother was standing on the other side of the ant river, holding a hurricane lamp to give light. His father came out of the kitchen and began to pour boiling water over the ants. Hundreds of ants were washed against the wall and died. Thousands perhaps. But in seconds the army formed up to replace the ants that had fallen and make the river whole again.

"Can we not get Mon-Gay to come and eat them?" said the boy.

"I don't think so," said his mother. She had jumped over the ant river and come to his door. "Mongooses don't like ants. Besides, Laurie is up at Jos for a few days and she's taken Mon-Gay with her in case of snakes."

Laurie lived in the village. She worked with the boy's father at the airfield. Mon-gay was her pet. She called him her bodyguard. The boy had seen Mon-Gay at work; seen him attack a cobra, a snake he'd been told had the fastest strike in Africa. Mon-Gay never lost a fight against a cobra, Laurie had told him.

In the morning when they got up, the hall carpet had a big hole in it, about three feet wide. His mother was sweeping up dead ants. She had already filled a bucket with them when the boy looked out of his door.

"They ate the carpet," said the boy. "The ants."

"Yes," his mother said. "It's what they do."

"We can get a new one at the market on the weekend," said his father from the kitchen.

"Usually the ants take their dead away with them," said his mother. She was speaking to the boy's father, who was still in the kitchen.

"Well, they've made a right mess," said the boy's father. "It would be helpful if they would come back and clean it up."

The boy's mother didn't answer.

"How could they take all the dead ants with them?" the boy said. "There must be a thousand of them."

"More like a million," said his father. He worked at the airport; he was good at making calculations.

"Wouldn't Mon-Gay eat the dead ones?" the boy said.

"I don't know. He might," said his mother. "But I'm not sure if he would. I know mongooses don't like ants when they're alive."

"Nonsense! Wherever did you hear that?" said the boy's father. "They eat ants. It's part of their diet."

"I know where they came from," the boy's father said at lunch the next day. It was a Saturday.

"Where?" said the boy. "How do you know?"

"Emille said they came from the biggest of the ant-hills across the road. I've arranged for a bulldozer from the airport to come and remove it."

"How does Emille know where they came from?" said the boy's mother.

"Emille tracked them. He showed me. They'd eaten everything in their path."

They heard the sound of a big diesel engine. The boy's father went out to watch. The noise went on for several minutes, punctuated with loud bangs.

"I want to go and look," the boy said.

"It's time for your nap," said his mother.

"Just for a few minutes. I promise I'll go to sleep afterwards."

She gave in and they went out the front door and walked to the fence and leaned on the front gate. Across the road, about thirty feet on the other side of it, a big yellow bulldozer was backing away from a big, red anthill. The anthill was spired and spiked in red laterite, like a sculpture of an ancient cathedral.

The bulldozer backed up ten feet and the driver lifted the enormous blade three or four feet off the ground and pitched the bulldozer forward. Written along the bulldozer's side in runny red paint was the name 'ESME'.

Esme crashed into the anthill and released a cloud of dust. Esme backed away. When the dust cleared the anthill was still there. The driver got down from Esme's cab and walked across the road to speak to the boy's father. The bulldozer was making a put-put-put noise and popping puffs of black smoke from its chimney.

"Dynamite," said the bulldozer driver. They were close enough for the boy and his mother to hear them. "It's the only way you're going to move it."

"You mean you can't knock it down with the bulldozer?" said the boy's father.

"Some of them you can't. This is an old one. They build these things with laterite, and they bind it all together with their saliva. You've got no idea how solid these things are. I can take out concrete with Esme here, but I can't always take out an ant-hill. Only about half the time."

"Do you know a good dynamite man?" asked the boy's father.

"The only one I know is working in Jos right now."

"That's a hundred and fifty miles away. Surely there's someone closer."

"I don't know of anyone else. The only one I know is the man who did the blasting for your airport, and he's in Jos."

The dynamite man came three days later. It was early in the morning when he knocked on the front door. His name was Kofi.

The boy's father was about to go to work. "I've got to leave for the airport in half an hour," he said.

"No matter," Kofi said. "I can do it by myself. Just show me what you want me to do. I was only told that you had a job for me."

The boy's father put on a pair of thick boots and they walked to the front gate. There was no traffic on the red-dirt road. Hardly anyone had a car in Kaduna then. The boy's father, who was English, only had an old truck, and it was owned by the airline company.

There were three big anthills, about twenty yards beyond the far side of the road. They were spaced apart, two of them quite close. The third one, perhaps fifty feet away, was the biggest.

"It's this one," said the boy's father, walking up to the one furthest from the others. It was taller than he was, with a wide circumference at its base. "This is the one the ants came from. The bulldozer couldn't knock it down."

"No," said Kofi. "It's an old one. A strong one, I can see. Are you sure this is it?"

"Yes. Emille tracked the ants here, and the bulldozer driver agreed it was where the ants had come from. I know the bulldozer driver from the airport. He had to remove anthills there last year so we could lay the runway matting. He knows what he's doing. I was surprised he couldn't knock it down with Esme, but he gave it a good try."

"Esme?"

"The bulldozer." He opened the door of the truck and climbed in. Before he drove away he called across to Kofi. "Make sure you don't break all my windows when you blow that thing up!" He gave a wave and then he was gone, up the road in a cloud of red laterite dust.

The boy stood at the gate and watched Kofi making his preparations. First Kofi took a flat-bladed pickaxe and bashed some indentations low down on the sides of the anthill. When he'd finished he took a whisk hanging on twine at his waist and brushed dust and laterite chips from where he had made the indentations.

The sun had climbed higher in the sky and the day was becoming hot. Kofi turned from the anthill and walked back across the road. His shirt was sticking to him and perspiration was running down his face and arms. The sweat had turned some of the laterite dust on his skin into mud.

"Before I start the drilling I would like a glass of water," he said. "Would you be kind enough to ask your mother for one and bring it to me?"

The boy went into the house. A few minutes later he came back with the water. Kofi drank it in one go and handed him the empty glass. "That's good," he said. "Thank you. All that dust made me thirsty."

"Why did you hit the anthill with a pickaxe?" the boy said. "The bulldozer couldn't knock it down. Did you think you could knock it down with the pickaxe?"

Kofi laughed. "Oh, well you can see how rough the surface of the anthill is. I need to prepare flat places so I can drill holes in it." He reached over the gate and pulled up a blue canvas bag he had brought with him. He opened the bag and brought out a big drill. It was round and silver-coloured, with a handle at its side. The drill-bit was a foot long. At the top of the drill a long piece of metal was flattened out at its end like the part of a crutch you would put under your arm. Layers of tape were wound round it to create padding. He slid the drill-bit in the chuck and tightened it, then he held the drill up and showed the boy how it worked by turning the handle.

"It's a very good drill," Kofi said. "It was made in America."

"Why do you want to drill holes in the anthill?" the boy said.

"I need to blow it up. In order to blow it up I need to sink three sticks of dynamite into it. If I place dynamite on its outside it won't work. The explosion would go the wrong way. It would probably break all the windows in your house."

"What's this part for?" said the boy, touching the padding at the top of the drill.

"Oh, that's so I can lean my chest against it and push it when I'm drilling. That way my weight helps the drill-bit bite into whatever it is I'm drilling into."

The boy didn't have any more questions. Kofi walked back across the road and soon the quiet was disturbed by the whirring of the drill-bit as it ate slowly into the anthill.

When the boy's father came home the anthill was gone. The other two anthills were standing where they had been, the last touch of sunlight red on their flanks. Kofi had gone too. The twilight was short in Kaduna. It would be dark in a few minutes. His father came into the boy's room and lifted the side of the mosquito net and kissed the boy lightly on the forehead.

"Sleep tight," he said. He stood up and lowered the mosquito net. "I'm going to go and have a beer now. I've been looking forward to it all day." The boy knew his father was referring to the Star beer in the fridge. "I don't think we'll have any more trouble from the ants. Your mum will come in to read you a story in a few minutes."

"I don't want the ants to come back," the boy said when his mother came to read to him. "There were too many of them. I didn't like them."

"They've gone now," his mother said. "They've gone to look for food. They won't come back."

"What about the other ants?"

"What other ants?"

"The ones in the other ant hills."

"I don't think there are any of them left over there dear. Emille said they all came from the one that's gone." She was sitting beside him under the mosquito net. She smoothed his hair back and pulled the bedsheet up under his chin. "It says in the bible that ants are one of four things which are very small upon the earth but are exceeding wise. They are not strong, but they work together to prepare their food in summer so they will have lots to eat in winter."

She looked down at him. His eyes were closed. He was fast asleep.

African Postscript

Years later the boy and his mother went back to West Africa. They were travelling to a different place from where they had lived when the boy was five. Now he was nearly fourteen, and nine years is a long time in a young life. One of the things his mother wanted was to try and find Emille, but since they were not going to Kaduna she didn't think it was possible.

The last year they had lived in Kaduna the old truck had broken down. It couldn't be fixed, so the company had arranged for the boy's father to have a driver who would transport him to work in the company's only car. The driver's name was Tallyboo. A different driver would drive the company's car when Tallyboo had a day off. The second drivers' name was Boshang.

The plane stopped to refuel in the Canary Islands. It was an overnight stop and the passengers were taken by bus from the airport to a hotel in Las Palmas. Early the next morning the bus took them back to the airport, and they took off for Bathurst, a thousand miles down the west coast of Africa. Today, Bathurst is called Banjul. It was hot when they landed there, even though it was well before noon. The aeroplane was refueled, and they took off for Freetown in Sierra Leone.

When the crew opened the aeroplane's cabin door at Freetown, it was as if they had opened the door to a blast furnace, the heat was so intense. The boy and his mother went down the steps onto the tarmac and then, quite suddenly, a tall man dressed in a neat brown suit, came running up to them. He stopped in front of the boy's mother and threw his arms around her in a great hug.

"Tallyboo!" she said. "This is wonderful." She hugged him back and held him out in front of her and studied his face. "It *is* you," she said. "I can't believe it. You haven't changed a bit in all those years." She hugged him again, as the other passengers filed past them at the bottom of the steps and made their way across the baking tarmac to the little air-conditioned terminal building.

Tallyboo told them he was still working for the company. He was its principal driver at Freetown. The only difference from Kaduna was that he had to wear a suit now, but the company paid him more. He laughed. "Who would think a suit would be worth more money. It didn't make me a better driver!"

Boshang, he said, lived in Bathurst. He didn't work for the company any more. He had saved up and bought a taxi, and that's how he made his living.

"Do you know where Emille is?" the boy's mother asked. "Have you heard anything about him?"

"Oh, not for many years," Tallyboo said. "He married a young woman called Atikah and they left Kaduna, but I don't know where they live."

The boy felt a tiny pang in his chest, and it went away. He didn't know where it had come from. The mention of Emille's name perhaps—because Emille had been kind and he had learned much from him. Emille had even taught him to speak Hausa. But, living in Britain since those days, he had lost the language. He didn't remember a word of Hausa now—except for that word 'Atikah'. Atikah, Atikah. What did it mean? He knew it must mean something. But what?

Warts

"*Senatus Populusque Romanus.* That is what SPQR means. It was on their battle standards, and on their coinage. It was etched into the monuments and the facades of buildings all over the Empire. It was *de facto*, the emblem of the state, of the republic itself. Along with the phrase *Civis Romanus Sum*—which embodied the right of the people they conquered to become Roman citizens—SPQR stood at the very root of the Romans' genius." He moved to his desk, breathing hard, his face flushed. "Once again, you have not done your homework."

I knew what he was going to do. He was going to open his desk and reach inside it for the strap. His name was Peate. Mr. Peate. We called him Boggy, as in peat bog. We didn't get on well. He was an awkward, cumbrous man. His tweed sports jacket with its leather elbow pads didn't button up properly at the front, and his shirt bulged in untidy folds over the top of his corduroy trousers.

Boggy lived in the basement apartment below the flat where we lived. He wore suede shoes, which my mother called 'brothel creepers', and he never paid the rent on time. He knew we didn't think much of things like that. My mother said he'd overheard her complaining about him to one of the neighbours. Perhaps that's why he took out his quiet anger on me. But I didn't understand any of that at the time. I was only twelve.

We knew that Boggy had been to Oxford University. He spoke about it often, and he once got cross when I pronounced Magdalen College the way it's spelled. Mag-da-len.

"Madelen," he shouted. "Mad-ell-en." He didn't go for the strap that time, but it didn't take much to send him off in that direction. He was different with the other pupils, but I knew that was probably because my mother and I were his landlords. We lived in the castle and he lived in the dungeon. My mother hadn't been to Oxford University, nor to any other university. But we had money that mother had inherited, and Boggy was a poorly paid teacher of a dead language.

The day of the SPQR was the day after the doctor had tried to freeze the warts on the palms of my hands. It was how they got rid of them then, by dabbing them with a substance that fizzed and hurt. Overnight my warts had ballooned into painful blisters. When I examined them that morning it looked as if there was blood inside one or two of them.

Boggy pulled out the strap and told me to come to the front of the class. "It's not because you're not intelligent," he said, employing a double negative as he liked to do. "It's because you're intellectually indigent. Bone lazy."

I didn't like pain at any time, but especially not then, after the wart removal 'cure' I'd had. I said, "Excuse me sir, but the doctor gave some treatments to my hands yesterday and they're quite painful today."

Boggy clearly thought I was trying to get out of a punishment. He didn't even look at my hands. "Nonsense boy," he said. "What you're about to get from me is an entirely different kind of treatment. It's something that will awaken your brain. A tonic I would call it. A stimulus. Be mindful of Winston Churchill's words at a time of crisis: 'We shall operate on the donkey at both ends, with a carrot and with a stick.'"

I had never seen the carrot in Boggy's class. Only the stick, which he uncoiled. It was a thick piece of leather, about three feet long. He swished it experimentally at the side of his desk in order to tune up the muscles of his thrashing arm. "Right hand first," he said. "Hold it steady with your left hand so it doesn't fall away."

The warts on my right hand were the worst ones. The doctor had applied the freezing device twice to each of them on that hand. The fizzing noise it had made as it burned the warts off had given me nightmares.

The problem came with the first hit. The strap broke two of the blisters and both of them were full of blood. The blood went all over Boggy's sports jacket and white shirt. It made him angry. He must have thought I'd played some kind of trick, perhaps by holding a small balloon filled with red ink in my hand.

"Left hand," he barked, and I held out my left hand.

The result was not as dramatic as it had been with the right hand, but it made almost as big a mess. The blood from the blisters on that hand hit him right in the face, a perfect TV murder-mystery blood spatter. Just then the door opened and in came the Headmaster. It took me a little while to figure out why the Head immediately grabbed me and marched me out of the classroom and off to his study. The strap hitting my left hand had hurt more than the one on my right hand, and I'd drawn it away and bunched it up in a fist to lessen the pain. To the Head it must have looked as if I'd punched Boggy on the nose. Whatever it was he thought, he called the police as soon as we got to his study. It took them less than five minutes to get there. They must have been passing down the street in a squad car.

"An assault is it then, sir?" said the first policeman. He looked at the blood on my hands. It had dripped onto my trousers and shoes, some of it onto the carpet in the Head's study.

"It is," said the headmaster. "The boy is trouble. He's punched one of our teachers. I saw it. Take him away please. I shall call his parents to come and pick him up at the police station."

"It doesn't work quite like that sir," said the first policeman. "We were not witness to what appears to have been an act of physical violence. You will have to lay a formal complaint before we can take custody of the boy and start the necessary paperwork for an assault charge." He pulled a notebook and a pen from his pocket. He looked around the Head's study while he was waiting, taking in the wide oak desk, the framed photographs of Prize Day and the school's sports teams on the walls.

The Head gave a short statement that the first policeman duly wrote down. The second policeman, who was younger, hadn't said a word. I knew the Head's statement wasn't true. He hadn't witnessed the strapping, hadn't seen how Boggy had got himself covered in blood. Neither policeman asked the Head questions about anything he said in his statement.

"It's not often we get called in to this school is it Bob? At this end of town it's more likely we get to sort out a rammy at the one down by the greyhound track."

They were escorting me to the police car. Neither of them had said a word to me; neither of them had asked me a question. Not even something basic like, "What can you say about what happened in that classroom?" Now they were chatting to each other as if I wasn't there.

"I don't think we've ever been called to this school," said the younger policeman. "At least, I've never been here before. It's for posh kids isn't it? People with money."

They put me in the back seat, and drove me up the hill to the police station. It had begun to rain. Nobody had asked if I wanted to get my coat, or collect any of my things. My jacket was still at my desk in the Latin class. Boggy had made me take it off before he strapped me. I was wearing grey shorts, a grey flannel shirt with a bit of blood spatter on it, and the blue and white school tie.

When we reached the police station the policemen took me inside, again without saying a word to me. The man behind the counter had three stripes on his arm. "What's this then," he said, indicating me. "Serious crime?"

"You could say that," said the first policeman with a small laugh. "It's an assault. He's bloodied his Latin teacher's nose. Still got blood on his hands. See?"

The sergeant's eyebrows went up, and he looked down at my hands. It seemed to me he was trying not to laugh. Instead he said, "All right. What's his name?"

They were talking around me. None of them had spoken directly to me. I was about to give my name when the first policeman said, "What's your name son?"

The desk sergeant spoke before I could answer. "Wait a minute. You're not telling me you've brought him in here and you haven't even taken his name yet."

"Sorry Sarge. We're just doing what his headmaster asked us to do. He's laid the complaint."

The sergeant shook his head, opened the blotter on the counter and picked up a pen. He looked at me. "Name and address," he said.

That was when the door burst open and Boggy came in, with blood spatters across the front of his shirt and the lapels of his jacket. He must have washed the blood from his face, but he was quite a sight. The Sergeant looked up, his pen poised an inch from the form on which he was about to enter my name and address.

"No, no," Boggy said. "There has been a terrible mistake." He was perspiring heavily, and greatly agitated. This was not the mean character I'd come to know who lived in the basement of our townhouse flat. "The boy is not at fault here. It was me; my fault."

The Sergeant looked him up and down, taking in the blood on Boggy's shirt. There was even blood on his suede shoes; the brothel creepers. He put down his pen and leaned on the counter. "You're not telling me that you inflicted those wounds on yourself," he said.

"There are no wounds on me," said Boggy. "Look at the boy's hands and you'll see where the blood came from. I was too stupid to understand it. Too quick to inflict the strap on him." He looked at me. "I am terribly sorry. Please accept my apology for what happened."

I didn't know what to say, but I didn't have time to say anything because events moved along quickly when my mother burst through the door of the police station.

"You little reptile," she said. "How could you have done such a cowardly thing? You should have taken your punishment like a man instead of lashing out at Mr. Peate. You have brought disgrace on your whole family."

"No. No," said Boggy. He looked at the police sergeant, then at my mother. "*Condemnant quo non intellegunt. Hoc malum possit esse quod factum est.*"[1]

The desk sergeant dropped his pen. The two policemen looked at Boggy, at my mother, and back at Boggy again. Nobody looked at me. I hadn't even remembered SPQR in the class; I had no idea what Boggy had said.

"You don't understand," Boggy said. He was looking at my mother, his landlady. "This is easily sorted out. The whole thing was entirely my fault."

It was a warm evening. The sun was going down behind the trees across the street, and I was just finishing my homework. Through the open window I heard a rattle of ice, and a chink of glasses coming together. I looked out of my bedroom window. Down below, on the little landing by our front door, my mother had set out the picnic table and two chairs. Boggy was sitting in one of them, my mother in the other. They raised their glasses to one another and drank, and my twelve-year-old mind reeled with unspeakable possibilities.

---

1. They condemn that which they do not understand. This wrong can be undone.

Kojo and the Robin

Kojo came in a hatbox on a flight from West Africa with the boy's mother. In the Hausa language Kojo is a word they use for 'coming together'. It's a friendly, positive word that's hard to translate precisely, but it means to gather in harmony.

He was a chatty bird, so the boy's mother had fed him brandy with an eye dropper to keep him quiet on the long flight to Britain. He wouldn't have been allowed into Britain if the Customs people had known about him—even then, long before we began to realise it was wrong to keep a wild bird like a West African Grey parrot in a cage.

Kojo was a sensation in Edinburgh with the boy's friends. He would let the bird out of his cage to wander around the house. He didn't like to see him cooped up. Sometimes he would take him into the garden. Kojo didn't have flight feathers; they had been clipped. They could grow back again if he was ever to be set free.

The boy knew he was in trouble when Kojo got in a fight with his mother's Venus Fly-Trap one day. His mother was a keen gardener, and it might have been the only Venus Fly-Trap in the city outside the Botanical Gardens. Kojo destroyed it. When the boy's mother came home it was in pieces, all over the floor in the conservatory. The boy's friend Max said the fly-trap must have been opening and closing its mouth, and Kojo had taken it as a challenge.

In summer when the boy took Kojo into the garden he would keep him in his cage. He didn't want the crows to attack him as they sometimes did with eagles in the Highlands. A few of the smaller local birds would fly down and hang about the cage. They had probably never seen a West African Grey before. After he'd spent a couple of weeks on daily excursions to the garden, Kojo was speaking blackbird, sparrow, and occasional crow.

Kojo had a persistent suitor, a robin redbreast. The boy didn't know whether it was a male robin or a female robin. Come to think of it, he didn't know if Kojo was male or female either. This robin would fly down and land on the lawn in front of Kojo's cage, and strut up and down like it was on parade. Kojo didn't say a word to it, he just watched. The robin would come by every time Kojo was in the garden. It seemed to the boy that they became friends. Then he heard Kojo talking to it in robin.

When it drew towards autumn and it became colder the boy stopped taking Kojo outside. The robin tracked him down, and the boy saw it pacing up and down on the window sill. It must have become annoyed that it couldn't hear Kojo responding to its entreaties, because one day it started flying at the window beside his cage. The first time the boy saw it was when his attention was taken by the scraping of the robin's claws across the glass. Soon the window was dirty with whatever the robin had on its feet. "Probably excrement," said Max when he was at the house one day.

"Excrement?" said the boy.

"Pooh," said Max.

It didn't stop. It got worse. The robin was incredibly persistent. It began to fly at the window like a dive-bomber and pull up at the last moment. Then it somehow figured out that it could evacuate its bowels at the same time. Its bomb-aimer accuracy was remarkable. Soon the whole window next to Kojo's cage was splattered with bird poop.

The boy's mother had a fit. "I told you not to take him outside," she said. "Now he's got the whole bird neighbourhood over-excited."

"It's not my fault," the boy said.

"Yes it is. You'll have to clean it up."

"And it's not the whole bird neighbourhood. It's just the robin."

"I don't care who it is, I want you to clean it up. We've got people coming to dinner tomorrow. I need it done by then."

The next morning the boy went out to clean the window with a bucket of soapy water and a sponge mop. He gave the glass a good scrub, and sluiced it down. It didn't deter the robin at all. It kept up its kamikaze missions for weeks, even after the boy's mother moved Kojo to another room and away from the windows.

When the robin hadn't been seen for a while the boy's mother relented and put Kojo back out in the conservatory. One day she went out to the shops and forgot to lock the front door. The boy was at school. When his mother came home there was no sign of Kojo or his cage. She called the police. When the boy came home from school there was a police car parked at the front door.

"It happens a lot," the policeman was saying when the boy walked into the kitchen. "These birds are valuable. There's a ready market for them." He turned to the boy. "Your mother says you were especially close to the bird. You don't know anything about this do you son?"

The boy shook his head. He didn't know if he was being accused of having something to do with Kojo's disappearance or not.

"Right," the policeman said. "We'll put the word out to the pet shops. Sometimes the thieves will try to sell it on; get some money for it."

The policeman left. "We'll never see Kojo again," said the boy's mother, "and it's all my fault. How could I have been so stupid, leaving the front door unlocked like that?"

When the boy's father came home he shook his head. "The police are far too busy to bother about a parrot," he said.

"They came to the house," said the mother. "The policeman said he would put the word out about Kojo. He said he thought they might be able to find him."

"Not a chance," the father said, and picked up the evening newspaper.

The mother was upset, but she wasn't one to sit around and do nothing. The next morning there was a story about Kojo in the newspapers. The headline was "Parrot Kidnapped". Beneath it there was a photograph of Kojo the boy's mother must have given them. The article wasn't on the front page, it was on page five, but it was several column inches long. At the end of it the newspaper asked its readers to keep an eye out for a West African Grey parrot in a local pet shop, or in someone's house who hadn't had a parrot last week.

Three or four days later the telephone rang. It was late on a Saturday afternoon. The boy's mother and father were out.

"We've found your parrot," said the voice on the other end. He gave his name as Constable MacDuff. "Will someone be home if I bring it round to your house?" He confirmed the address and hung up.

The policeman brought Kojo to the house an hour later. The boy thanked him, and the policeman left. The boy chatted away to Kojo as he always did, but Kojo never said a word. He just looked depressed. Sullen. Apart from the bird languages, he'd had a good vocabulary before he'd been stolen; phrases like "I yam a talking parrot", and "What's your game, sonny?" He would infuriate the boy's father by imitating the ringing of the telephone, and some of the boy's friends had taught him words he shouldn't have said. But that morning the boy couldn't get Kojo to say anything at all. He wouldn't even bob his head up and down like he did when he was pleased to see people.

The boy was ready to give up when the telephone rang. It was someone from the *Daily Mail*. He identified himself as a crime reporter.

"I hear you got your parrot back," he said. "Where did they find him?"

"The policeman said they found him in a pet shop at Bruntsfield," the boy said.

"Which one?"

"I don't know. The policeman didn't say."

The reporter sighed at the other end of the phone. "Right, I'll see what I can find out. How's he doing?"

"He seems a bit fed up," the boy said. "He hasn't said a word since the police brought him home."

"Oh, he speaks does he?"

"Normally he does. But he's just sitting on his perch now with his feathers all fluffed up. I can't get him to say anything."

The reporter asked a few more questions and hung up. There wasn't much for him to write about.

The next morning at breakfast the boy's father opened the newspaper. "Oh, for Pete's sake," he said. He turned the page round so his wife and son could see it.

"Parrot Silent after Kidnap Ordeal" was the headline. It was plastered in black type across the top of page three. The reporter had injected some humour into the story, and his readers probably got a laugh from it.

A week after that the robin was back. The boy couldn't see it when he looked out the window, but he recognised its idiotic voice right away. Then the telephone rang. The boy picked it up but there was nobody there, just the dial tone. A minute later the robin started up again. It was in the conservatory.

The Doodlebug

The sky was late-summer blue, pale and empty but for dollops of fluffy cumulus. The boy's grandmother was standing beside him, her feet planted on the crazy-paving garden path.

"That's the way they came," she said, pointing at a white cloud. "From the south. Behind the fence." She reached out with gnarled, arthritic fingers, twisting her hand as if she was grasping for something. "Doodlebugs."

"Were there many of them?" said the boy. He was fourteen. He had heard of them.

She turned her good ear towards him.

"Were there many of them?" he said, more loudly.

"Oh yes. Oooh, my goodness, yes." Her voice cracked. "It was all right as long as you could hear them. They made a puttering noise. Loud. Like your Grandad's old motorbike. But . . ." She sighed and looked away. "You wouldn't remember that." She lost herself in thought.

After a minute he touched her arm. "You said it was all right if you could hear them."

"Yes. As long as you could hear them everything was all right. When the noise stopped you had to watch out. That was the frightening part. The quiet."

She regarded a clump of thistles in the rose bed. "They wouldn't be there if your Grandad was still alive." She turned to look at her grandson. "When the noise stopped they fell down. When the noise stopped we had to run for the air raid shelter." She waved her hand at the rose bed. "There was ever such a bang when they landed. The one that came down up at Chilton's farm broke all the windows in the street. Every one of them." She frowned. "Chilton's farm's nearly a mile away."

"Where was the air raid shelter?" he said. He was puzzled sometimes by the intensity with which his Gran spoke about things that had happened so long ago.

She gestured at the roses. "It was right there, where the roses are. We dug a big hole and put it there." She looked at her hands, thinking of the labour that had gone into it. "I didn't like it one bit. It was damp. After the war your Grandad thought he could grow mushrooms in it." She stopped for a moment. "But he never did."

"It would have made a good gang hut," said the boy. "Or you could have used it as a garden shed."

"Too damp," she said. "The lawnmower would have rusted." She looked over at the coal bunker which stood by the back door. "The breeze blocks there; we used them for the air raid shelter. We put a corrugated roof on top of them and built earth up its sides." She pointed at the ramshackle lean-to which served as a toolshed. "The door frame for that was the door to the air raid shelter."

The boy knew his father had been a pilot in the war, knew he'd gone from grammar school to work in a bank for a year, that when the war had come his application to join the Air Force had been accepted. The boy had been told of weeks of training at a remote airfield in the north of Scotland, where it had rained and rained. He'd been told nothing about the rest of it.

His father had been sent to a squadron that flew big, four-engined bombers. Losses on the squadron had been high. Only a few of the others at the base had even asked his name. Some of them saw no point in it. The average bomber crew lasted only seven operations, and he had to do thirty. His first raid had been to Essen in Germany's Ruhr Valley, and the anti-aircraft fire had been bad. There had been no clouds, and a slice of moon had given the German gun crews all the light they'd needed. He'd made his bomb run in a stupor of fear, and violent coloured lights bursting in front of him.

On the way home they'd been caught over Holland by a night-fighter, and when the rear gunner shouted for him to take evasive action he'd kicked at the rudder bar and missed, and the aeroplane had started a slow, flat turn instead of corkscrewing as he'd been taught to do. It had taken only a moment to correct the mistake, but it had been too long for the rear gunner. It had cost him his life.

Flying home in the half-light of early morning, he'd seen ghost trees poking through the mist above the Lincolnshire fens, the noise of the slipstream wind spiraling through the shattered gun turret loud in his earphones, emphasising the silence of the dead rear gunner. He'd switched off the bomber's systems when they landed, and watched the sun pink over the fields, give colour to the grey ground mist, and make diamonds of the water droplets on the bomber's windscreen. Then he'd climbed down from the cockpit to see his navigator vomiting by the bomber's tail. He'd stood as the ground crew hosed the dead gunner out of the turret, and watched the essence of the man flow down the side of the broken fuselage onto the ground. He'd been a good gunner, conscientious, and part way through his second tour of operations. 'Lucky Len', the crew had called him, and it had come to this.

It had not been the end of it. The boy's father had been given another bomber and a new rear gunner, and he'd gone out again two nights later. The next seven operations had cost five more crew members—a wireless operator, a flight engineer, two more gunners, and a navigator. It was a long way from Lucky Len. Whisperers on the base began to speak of the boy's father as Jonah.

The boy knew none of these details. He'd been told his father was twenty-two years old when he'd started flying, and that he'd been away from home for eight months before they gave him any leave. The longest he'd ever been away before that was a camping trip to the South Downs on a bank holiday weekend.

"He was confused by the muddle of it. Your father. The madness," his grandmother had told him after his grandfather had died, filling an emptiness in the circle of knowledge. "The peaceful countryside before he had to get in his aeroplane, and an hour later they were all twisted up in the sky. Searchlights hunting them. Bombs bursting. Cities on fire. The smell of it. The noise," and the boy remembered a tear on her cheek.

The day the boy's father had walked up the hill from the railway station to his parent's house at the start of his leave, the street had looked the same as it had always looked; a small, semi-detached corner of peace and safety. The Luftwaffe had paid little attention to this part of south, suburban London, even though it lay on a direct route from France to the centre of the city.

After three days his nerves had begun to relax. The garden was producing more vegetables than he remembered. He'd never paid much attention to his father's plantings, but he noticed that flower beds of dahlias and gladioli had been usurped by rows of cabbage and lettuce, and runner beans were growing in a wide screen at the top of the garden. Close to the house the rose bed was gone, replaced by the ugly corrugations of an Anderson shelter, with chalky grey soil banked up against its sides.

He'd been quiet, saying little to his father, less to his mother. Even his friend Tom, home on a break between convoy escorts, was unable to get much out of him. But on the fifth day of his leave he'd begun to do some work in the garden. He mowed the lawn, savouring the scent of grass cuttings, and the rattle of the ratchet as he drew the mower back. An afternoon in the late summer sunshine made him happy; shirt off, weeding among the vegetables while his father tied up the runner beans. The dirt etched into the pores of his skin gave him a sense of strength.

The last evening of his leave he had a conversation with his father about the local football team. No, his father agreed, the football wasn't as good as it had been before the war. The best players had gone into the forces. But it was good that the league continued; good for morale. It wasn't much of a conversation, but it eased the tension in the house.

The air raid sirens had sounded that night. His parents had quickly snatched up blankets, a jug of water, and sandwiches his mother made every day, just in case. She had just made a pot of tea and she took it with her to the shelter. Their son followed slowly. He'd inspected the shelter the day he'd come home, and he hated the dampness and claustrophobia of it. Six feet long and five feet wide, it was cramped, and it smelled of a crypt. He made his way to it through the up and down of the sirens as if he was ploughing through thick, wet sand.

He wedged himself into a corner in the only shadow left by the candle light, and sat with his eyes closed, his arms folded across his chest, his fingers digging into his flesh as the ground shook with the percussion of bombs. The candle flickered and went out, the noise of the sirens coming from inside his own head, and he thought of the people in the cities below his bomber. People with the same fear pricking their skin, dampening their armpits, and he understood that they would curse him to hell as he flew three miles above their heads. He smelled his sweat and saw himself staring down from the loud cockpit of his bomber, and heard the sirens sounding for him.

The boy set out sticks to make a cycle course around the undulations at the recreation ground. He'd been given a stop watch for his birthday, and he spent the afternoon timing himself round and round the cycle course. It had been a good idea, he thought, for the council not to level the ground when they had filled in the bomb crater. A hooded crow flapped over the fence from the corn field. The boy stood in soft sunshine and watched it fly towards Chilton's barn, and it was as if he had been in that place at another time; as if he was there now, and not there. As if there was knowledge just out of reach.

He rode his bike until the sun began to drop blood-red through a haze of garden bonfires. A line of Lombardy poplars stood black across the valley, like sentinels against the dying of the light. Far down the valley four tall chimneys poked over a corner of the Surrey downs; old, Elizabethan chimneys of a great house known as Caine Hill. He would always take a roundabout route home rather than walk the wooded lane past the old house after the sun had set. The place frightened him. He wasn't sure why, except one of his friends had said mad people lived there.

When he reached his grandmother's house he went to the garden shed to put some oil on the bicycle chain. He turned when he felt a gust of cold air as he opened the door. Nothing was there. No wind ruffled the leaves of the privet hedge. He lifted the back wheel of the bicycle and turned the pedals and squirted oil on the chain. Since his grandfather had died it was his job to fill the coal scuttle each evening. He lifted the lid of the bunker, and thrust the shovel into the coal. Another gust of cold air blew the hair at the back of his neck, so sudden that he almost dropped the scuttle. Again, he looked around. Again, nothing was there.

That night he dreamed; dreams with colours and scent. The subtle scent of springtime daffodils in Silver Lane, flowering privet. The musty smell of wet chalk soil after a rain. Woodsmoke from autumn bonfires. The colours at the recreation ground by Chilton's Farm were in his dreams too, and the strange textures and hues among the undulations at the top end of the field where the flying bomb had exploded. The grass there was never as green as the other grasses at the farm. It would turn coarse and brown before midsummer, as if the moisture had been sucked from the soil and left the grass to die.

Then the boy saw a young man in his dream. He was standing in front of the fireplace in the living room, holding his hands behind his back, shoulders hunched forward. He was wearing a blue shirt, black tie, blue uniform.

His grandmother was standing in front of the French window, indistinct, the sun bright through the window, distorting the outline of her.

"Do you know who this is?" she said.

"No," he whispered.

The man at the fireplace didn't move, said nothing.

"It's your father," she said, and raised her arm and pointed.

The man looked back at him, but his expression didn't change.

The boy woke up. He knew who the man was in the dream. His photograph was on top of the piano. The man by the fireplace had been a ghost.

It was dark and he could hear his grandmother in the next room, whimpering softly in her sleep, like a child. The dream had frightened the boy, but he didn't want to tell his grandmother about it. He got up and crept downstairs, taking care to miss out the third step because it would creak. He took a bunch of keys from a hook in the kitchen, and quietly climbed back up the stairs.

His father's old room was at the top of the house. It had always been kept locked. He'd been told he wasn't to go in there; that it was a storage room now. One of the keys opened the door of it. He turned on the light, and saw a small, single bed, a stuffed leather armchair with a white, woollen blanket folded over its back, and a dressing table with a mirror. A photograph of his father's aeroplane sat there; one of the early colour photographs, faded to a washed-out grey. A tall wardrobe stood in a corner, books piled on its top. He could make out some of the titles. "The Airship Golden Hind", and "Biggles Flies West". A window looked out at the garden, but it was closed, the garden was dark, and the air in the room was lifeless and old.

Then it seemed to him that he heard the dreadful sound of the doodlebug churning across the sky, and he turned off the light and went to the window and stared into the dark, and saw its short stubby wings, and the red, guttering flame from its engine. He heard the silence when the engine stopped, and watched it tumble over and over until it crashed in Chilton's field at the place where he had his time-trial bicycle track.

At breakfast he sat with his grandmother in front of boiled eggs and toast.

"What happened to him?" he asked.

"To whom?"

"To my father. What happened to my father? You never speak about him."

She stopped buttering the toast and looked up. "We've told you, dear. You know what happened to him."

The boy had no memory of it. "Tell me again," he said. "I want to know."

His grandmother put the knife down. The lenses of her spectacles caught the ceiling light. "He was killed in the war," she said. "The war killed him."

"How was he killed? Tell me what happened."

"He was in the Air Force. He died near the end of the war. Shot down one night." She picked up the knife and began to butter the toast again. "He had a lot of friends. They came to the service at the church. His crew came too."

"You've never told me that."

She put the knife down, and stood up and went to the piano. She reached for the photograph and ran her sleeve lightly across the glass. "No," she said. "You're fourteen now. Perhaps you're old enough to understand."

She stared through the lace curtains at the street. "He was a good man, your father. Very generous." She took off her spectacles and rubbed her eyes. "He liked music. I hear you playing his records on the gramophone sometimes. It makes me think of him. He liked to read too. You've read some of his books. 'Wind in the Willows'. 'William the Pirate'."

"How could his crew have gone to the service at the church? Weren't they killed too?"

His grandmother turned from the window and the boy watched as she looked at another photograph, this one on the mantelpiece. It was a wedding group, the picture browning with the years since it had been taken. It showed his aunt and uncle, with the boy's father in his air force uniform standing beside them.

"He was the best man," said his grandmother. "We were all so young then." She turned and sat down again. "He was very brave, your father." She cleared her throat. "But he wasn't the same after he joined the Air Force. Not the same."

"After he joined the Air Force?"

She cleared her throat again. "After his experience in the Air Force. It affected him. His letters changed. They were different, distant. They weren't allowed to come home. We didn't see him for months. Not even on weekends. Not when they were flying. We never knew where he was; what he was doing. It was all censored."

She looked at him and her eyes were big through the lenses of her spectacles. "We only saw him when he came home on leave. He wasn't the person we'd known. We could tell he wasn't well. He hardly said a word at first, although he perked up a little after a few days." She wiped her glasses on her apron, and put them back on her nose. "But then we had to spend the night in the air raid shelter. George and I could see he didn't like that, even when the bombing was far away."

The boy had never questioned what he'd been told. He had friends who had lost parents in the war. It was something you had to accept. There was nothing you could do about it. But now his grandmother was saying things he hadn't heard before.

"Then the doodlebug came over," she said. "We hadn't seen anything like it before. When it went off it made ever such a loud bang. It frightened us. They were always doing things to frighten us. They even put little propellers on their ordinary bombs so they would make a screeching noise. They didn't just want to kill us with the bombs; they wanted to frighten us to death." She picked up another piece of toast, and drew her buttering knife back and forth across it.

"They made a horrible noise, the doodlebugs. We didn't know what they were. We'd never heard them before that night. And then the noise stopped, and there was silence, and we thought they'd gone away."

She frowned. "But they hadn't. It wasn't until later, when there were more of them that we started to pray for the noise to continue." She leaned forward and peered at him. "I don't like to say it but we didn't feel bad wishing them on someone else."

"What did it look like Gran?" he said.

Lost in long-ago thoughts she looked up. "What?"

"The doodlebug. What did it look like?"

"Oh, it was ever such an evil-looking thing. They were black. They made a nasty black trail across the sky, and they were on fire at the back. They looked just like a . . . a doodlebug." She pointed. "They always came that way. Over the top of the garden."

Something caught her eye and she turned to look out the side window. "Mr. Howarth is late this morning," she said.

The boy turned in his chair and saw a portly, middle-aged man coming out of the house across the road. He was wearing a suit and a bowler hat, and carrying a rolled umbrella.

"He was a friend of your father's," she said, and the boy knew his father could not have grown old like Mr. Howarth.

His grandmother hummed softly as she poured tea from an old brown teapot. She put the teapot down, and put her hand to her chest and watched Mr. Howarth's back for a moment, retreating down the street. She took a deep breath.

"The night the doodlebug came he left the air raid shelter and went outside," she said. "George and I thought he'd just got a bit of claustrophobia. You know, being used to being up above the bombs and all. It must have been different for him, being cooped up on the ground. We thought he just needed to be out in the open air. Where there was space." She lifted her cup and took a sip of tea. The cup rattled against the china saucer when she put it down.

"George and I stayed in the shelter until the All Clear sounded. We didn't know then that he'd run up to his room. Do you want some more tea?"

The boy shook his head. It felt as if there was a hole in his stomach.

"We knew he wasn't well," she said. "We knew what he'd been doing was dangerous; that it had affected him. His letters had had to pass through the censors. They didn't tell us how he was, what he was thinking. They weren't allowed to say anything like that. He never told us where he was or what he was doing." She looked away to the net curtains and the houses across the road. "They were just . . . just far-away letters."

The clock ticked on the sideboard. A car drove up the street. The telephone rang in the next room, but she paid it no attention.

"He'd gone up to his room and locked the door." Her voice had faded, and the boy had to lean forward to hear her. "We couldn't get it open. He wouldn't answer us. In the end your Grandad and Mr. White the Air Raid Warden had to break it down." Her shoulders were shaking, her head bowed. "He isn't dead, you know."

The boy was still, his senses stopped, a buzzing in his ears. His heart was thumping. It was difficult to breathe.

"He lives near here," his grandmother said. "Perhaps I could take you to see him sometime." She looked at him over the top of her spectacles. "You're very like him." She turned to the net curtains again, her eyes faraway. "He was such a fine young man."

Queenie

Queenie wore black most of the time; perhaps all the time. It's the only colour I see her in now. Black skirt, black jacket, sometimes a black sweater; once, a white blouse. But only once. Black hair with a streak of white. Red lipstick, pale face; sitting behind her desk.

I don't remember Queenie's proper name. I don't think I ever knew it. She was just . . . Queenie; it's what everyone called her. She must have been in her fifties when I went north. She was not married.

I was warned about Queenie when they told me I was being posted to Aberdeen. They said she was the one who did all the work, all the planning, kept the books in order; that she was devoted to Mr. B, the theatre manager, that she covered for him when he went on a bender.

"She's fierce," they said. "A right battleaxe. The other trainees who've been up there have all said she gets out the wrong side of bed every morning. It's not like it is here in Edinburgh. You've got to toe the line or else she'll chew you into little bits and spit you out."

The first thing I did when I got to Aberdeen was buy myself a little medallion. I'd always wanted a Saint Christopher, but no one had ever given me one; not for my birthday, or for Christmas. In the end I couldn't find one I liked, so I settled for a plain silver disc. I wanted the jeweler to engrave "Good Luck Luke" on the back of it, but there wasn't room so I settled for "Luck Luke". It was a bit alliterative, but it was all the protection I could afford.

Queenie *was* fierce. Stern. She didn't seem to like people she didn't know, and she was tough. She didn't know me; didn't seem to want to. But that was fine. I was eighteen, and she was an old lady. Old people were just, well, old. It's how young people still look at old people, I think.

I'd been up there about a month when things took a strange turn. One Saturday morning after I'd helped out with the weekend Kid's Klub—cartoons, an adventure serial about the South Seas, and a couple of on-stage announcements—I couldn't find a pencil to reconcile the concessions chart. Sums were never my strong suit, and I needed to use a pencil so I could erase the mistakes I knew I'd make. The kids went through a lot of ice cream and chocolate, and the sales had to match the money we'd taken in, and that had to match the stock which had been sold out of the inventory we kept in the storeroom. There would be nicely sharpened pencils in Queenie's desk, and that's how I came across an old newspaper cutting when I was looking in one of her drawers.

CEYLON CYCLONE PASSES OUT TO SEA
Considerable Damage on Coast
(From Our Special Correspondent in Colombo)
Weather conditions throughout Ceylon show a distinct improvement today. The cyclone expected yesterday missed Colombo and is believed to have passed back out to sea. Considerable damage, however, is reported from lower down the coast, and at Bentota the rest-house was blown down. The floods, though general up-country, are not likely to affect Colombo or the low country, as little rain has fallen near the source of the Kelani river, which flows into Colombo. Information regarding the state of the railway is meagre owing to telegraphic breakdowns, but it will be some time before full service can be recommenced. Up-country mails will not run for several days.

The report was dated December 17, 1948. It struck me as odd, a slip of newspaper, neatly cut and trimmed and many years old, about a weather event on the other side of the world, lying in an office drawer in Aberdeen.

I still couldn't find a pencil so I looked in a filing compartment on the left side of Queenie's desk. A big piece of thick, folded paper dropped out when I opened the flap. The paper fell open when it hit the floor. It was a beautiful old poster. In gentle colours it showed palm fronds and a thatched hut, a dirt track, and an ox cart with a dark-skinned driver. Above the scene a little propeller-driven airliner sat in a blue sky. Etched across the top of the poster in red were the words "Fly to Ceylon by B.O.A.C.", except the B.O.A.C. part was in white script. For some reason I turned it over. On the back, in faded pencil, were the words *"I am become life; creator of worlds."* Beneath it were the initials BG, and a question mark.

Eventually I found a broken pencil in a drawer in Mr. B's desk. It was lodged under a flat, half-empty bottle of Buchanan's whisky. But the newspaper clipping and the Ceylon poster stayed in my mind. I knew Queenie's handwriting, and she hadn't written those words on the back of that poster. Someone else had.

Seven years before, when I was twelve, I'd flown out to Ceylon to see my father who worked there for that same British airline. I'd stayed at his house in Colombo for a month during the Easter holidays, and during that month he'd taken me down the west coast road to the beautiful, gold-sand beach at Bentota. We'd spent a day there, paddling in the salt-sea, lazing about, drinking fresh coconut milk, and eating sweet mango fruit. Later, before we drove back up the coast, he'd allowed me a small glass of Lion beer he bought at a little beach-side stall. I'd never been allowed to have beer before, and I never forgot it.

On the Monday I wanted to ask Queenie about the poster and the newspaper clipping, but I was afraid to. I didn't want her to think I'd been rummaging about in her desk on her day off. A week went by, and then another, and slowly I was accepted into that office; trusted to open up in the morning and close the theatre down at night; trusted to handle the bigger reconciliations and deposits, not just the pennies from the Kid's Klub on Saturday mornings.

The mark on Queenie's wrist was very small; an exquisite series of curves. It looked like the outline of a magic lamp. No, it was more elusive than that; more like the smoke from the magic lamp. It was a soft gold colour on the underside of her arm, just above her wrist. I saw it when she reached for a folder on her desk and the sleeve of her blouse pulled up a few inches.

I was intrigued. It was strange, exotic. It didn't fit the image of the Queenie I'd been warned about, or even the one I'd come to know. But I didn't really know her at all.

"It's beautiful," I said.

Queenie quickly pulled the cuff of her blouse down to hide it. Later I realised the look she had given me had meant she didn't want to talk about it.

"It's just a tattoo," she said.

"What does it mean?" With my under-financed explorations into St. Christopher ending up with my little 'Luck Luke' medallion, I was interested. Perhaps Queenie had taken a different route to protection from the one I'd taken.

"It's complicated," she said.

"It's a kind of symbol surely. What's it called?" I didn't think I was intruding. I was just curious.

Queenie sighed. It sounded like impatience. "Ichthys," she said.

I wasn't sure I'd heard her properly. I asked her to say it again.

"Ichthys," she said. She took out a pencil and a piece of paper and wrote 'ἰχθύς'. I stared at it, then at Queenie.

"In English it's spelled 'I-C-H-T-H-Y-S'."

I tried to say it the way Queenie had said it. "Ichthys," but I couldn't say it like she had. "It looks oriental," I said.

"Yes, I suppose it does, but it's actually not." She pulled back the sleeve of her blouse to show me. In that moment it seemed like an enormous confidence, as if she had shown me a secret part of her body.

"It's Hellenistic," she said. "Greek. It's very old, thousands of years old. In time it became a secret Christian symbol—an acronym in times when Christianity was banned. In America some people have stickers of it on their cars to show they're religious. The design they use isn't as attractive a depiction of the ἰχθύς as this one. It's rounder, more uniform." She paused. "More . . . regimented."

She turned away and pulled out the accounts ledger. I got the message that the conversation was closed, but it was so out of keeping with the warnings I'd been given in Edinburgh about her, that it made me think.

The next Saturday I picked up something odd from Mr. B when we were standing in the lobby in our evening wear, greeting the patrons. The theatre was showing a war film—Second World War. It was called 'The Victors'. It had some big stars in it, but it had been made by Carl Foreman, one of the Hollywood directors who had been black-listed in the United States after the anti-communist McCarthy hearings in the nineteen-fifties. The House un-American Activities Committee hadn't liked his answers to McCarthy's standard question, "Are you or have you ever been, a member of the Communist Party . . ."

Mr. B must have already had a few shots from his bottle of Black and White. "They never make films about the secret war," he said to me, as he nodded to a cinema-goer who was walking past. "Battle scenes. Saccharine stuff. That's what they give you. They never show the blood, the missing bits and pieces; arms and legs, people with their faces shot off. The mental cases. A film like this doesn't give you a sense of what it was really like."

'The Victors' had been done in Black and White—like Mr. B's whisky. The Producer hadn't been able to raise enough money for colour because of the Director's reputation. I'd seen the film and I thought it was pretty good. It had a message, a morality to it. Stupidity I suppose. The futility of war. One of the best scenes had shown a soldier being led out onto the white expanse of a frozen lake and tied to a post, and shot—for desertion, or cowardice, or something like that. It was a bleak, midwinter scene. No words, just Frank Sinatra singing 'Have Yourself a Merry Little Christmas' in the background as the firing squad raised their guns and killed him.

"Were you in the army then?" I said. "During the war?"

"Not the regulars, no," said Mr. B. "Other spheres. Overseas. Don't like to talk about it."

Secret war, he'd said. Overseas. "Where were you involved with it then?" I said. All the young people were fascinated by it in those days. The war. I was no different.

"Far East," he said. That was when he turned away and went back up to the office.

The conversation must have awakened something in him because we had to send Mr. B home early that night. It wouldn't do for the departing patrons to have seen him staggering around the lobby on their way out. Queenie called a taxi to come and get him, and from the conversation she had on the telephone I realised it was not an unusual occurrence.

Queenie must have taken pity on me because long after Mr. B had gone home, and after we'd done the reconciliations at the end of the evening, she asked if I would like to come to her flat for supper the next day. Sundays were a day off for us, and since I didn't have anything else to do I said I would, and what could I bring.

"Just bring yourself," she said. "Seven o'clock. Is that all right?"

I told her it was, and she gave me her address.

That Sunday morning I woke up in the bedsit I shared in Rosemount with Willie Crabbie to find a hard frost on the carpet of our room. It was the coldest winter they'd had in Aberdeen for years. The room was only warmed with a one-bar electric heater that worked on a meter we had to put money in. We'd get an hour for a shilling. It bought just enough time, sometimes, to get to sleep. But the cold wasn't the whole story. Willie was as broke as I was, and his solution to poverty was to save up milk bottles and take them along to the dairy and collect tuppence for each one. He'd keep the empties in his cupboard until he had enough of them to make the bus journey worth his while; a calculation that balanced the bus fare with the financial return. The problem was that Willie never bothered to rinse the empty bottles, and the room stank of sour milk. He kept the cupboard locked, probably in case I robbed him of his bottles, with the result that I couldn't get in there to wash them out myself.

That evening I walked down the hill from the bedsit, and through the gardens at Union Terrace. From there I made my way along Union Street, past our theatre, to the Mercat Cross in the oldest part of the city. Queenie had a small flat on Castle Street, where they'd held market days for centuries. It was just round the corner from the Gallowgate, where they used to hang people. There were no entry-phones in those days and I pushed the main door open and climbed up four flights of stairs. The stair smelled of the Saturday night just past, when the patrons of the bar at the corner must have used it as a lavatory on their way home.

There was no name on any of the doors on the top floor, but I knew which one was Queenie's. There were three doors on the top floor landing and she'd told me hers was the one on the left. That, and Queenie's door was painted black. The other doors were blue.

Queenie had gone to a lot of trouble over the meal. I don't think she would have earned much more than I did, and that wasn't much, but she served up a stout Cock-a-leekie soup, followed by a grilled salmon fillet with potatoes and peas. The Cock-a-leekie had chunks of chicken in it as well as leeks, carrots, and barley. It was delicious. Perfect for a winter night. Chicken wasn't cheap then. In our house in Edinburgh it had been a special treat. I maybe got chicken once a month when I lived there. Salmon wasn't cheap either. I knew that because I never saw it at home. Most of the salmon came from the rivers then; not from the sea. The Aberdeen trawlers caught fish that the fish-and-chippers preferred—haddock, cod, and occasionally halibut. The fish and chippers never served salmon.

I told Queenie I liked her cooking. Loved it actually. I couldn't believe a woman who could cook like that didn't have a husband, but I didn't say that.

She asked me what I normally did for meals. "Do you do your own cooking, or do you normally eat out?"

"I don't know how to cook," I said, "except I can do a boiled egg. I used to cook one up for my Mum on Sunday mornings and take it through to her on a tray with toasty soldiers and a cup of tea."

"Do you still do that for your Mum?"

"No," I said. "She's not there anymore. She's in Africa with my stepfather."

Queenie nodded and looked down at her plate. She hadn't given herself nearly as much as she'd served up for me. I said, "I think you've given me too much. You've got very little. Can I not give you some of mine?"

"No, thank you," she said. She was very thin, and I thought she looked a little sad. "This is more than enough for me."

It occurred to me that maybe she was sad because I'd mentioned Africa. I dearly wanted to ask her about Ceylon, but there was no easy way to do that. Then, suddenly I had a brainwave.

"It's funny," I said. "My Mum's in Africa, and my Dad's in India."

"Really? Where are they in those places? Do you know?" she said.

"My Mum's in West Africa; in Accra. My Dad is in Colombo," I said.

"Colombo's not in India." She said it right away, and I thought her voice had a bit of sharpness. "It's in Ceylon. It's a different country. It was never part of India; the Sri Lankan people are not the same." She looked at me. "They're mostly Buddhist. Most people in India are Hindi."

"Have you been there?" I said. It was the opening I wanted. I couldn't resist it.

Queenie looked down at her hands, and there was a touch of colour in her face, a slight flush.

"Yes," she said softly, "but it was a long time ago."

"Gosh, that must have been exciting. I liked it there. Loved it. It was a brilliant place." It was a chance for me to share something with her about my trip to see my father—and with my curiosity, I blew it. "What were you doing there?"

She looked up, and her eyes had narrowed, her face pale again. Queenie from the office. "It's not something I like to talk about," she said.

Mr. B. had said the same thing, not quite word for word. I felt a little embarrassed, but I couldn't do anything about it. My evening with Queenie came to an end, and as I walked back up to Rosemount I kicked myself for not taking a more considerate approach. You see, it seemed to me that whatever she had said at dinner about not wanting to talk about Ceylon, it was something she actually *did* want to talk about. I just hadn't been the right person.

As I pushed open the gate to the bedsit it occurred to me that perhaps it just hadn't been the right time. Maybe there wasn't even a right person in Aberdeen either; not someone who would understand. Not someone who had actually been there. That would be important. I had been to West Africa and to Ceylon, and I'd discovered that there's a magic in the air in the tropics. Magic can turn one's mind. Not only that, it's not something you can explain, because it needs all your senses to try and understand it. My mind took off with the thought of it.

The alchemy of the tropics lies in subtle things like the milk-sharp scent of sandalwood on my shirts after the dhobi in Colombo had washed and ironed them. That scent was hidden until I pulled open the drawer in my bedroom and released the most extraordinary sensation, all wrapped up in the smell of my shirts. It was a distillation of something I had never experienced before; a buzzing in my head like a thousand bumble bees or a hundred birds singing. That was just one thing I got from the tropics; a sense of vision that entered through my nostrils.

There was much more. It came flooding back—like the jerky film we'd shown the Kid's Klub about how they drew cartoons on bits of paper, and fanned them to create a sense of motion. I heard again the rhythmic drumming of a tropical rain on the roof, and saw the flash-flash-flash of sheet lightning which was like the greatest fireworks show in the world. The flowers in my father's garden in Colombo were such a storm of colour they had made me blink. The eiderdown wind running up and down the skin on my arm and on my bare legs was like what cats must feel when you stroke them; when they arch their backs to show their pleasure. The immaculate, imposing figure of M'habbia telling me, kindly, not to practice my climbing on the abstract-patterned, open cinder-block wall by the front door. The smell of baking bread in Cookie's little biscuit-tin oven in the enclosed yard where he made meals for my father and me, was unlike any smell I came across when I walked past the corner bakery on Mount Street. You couldn't buy anything like Cookie's biscuit-tin bread in Scotland.

Those things were all part of the enchantment; little bits and pieces of every day that added up to something that had been far beyond my imagination before I'd been to Ceylon. Where do you begin with any of that? Where does it stop? There was no one to talk to about it. Certainly not my mother. You didn't speak to parents about things like that; things you couldn't explain. None of my friends in Edinburgh understood it. Sensations like that were impossible to capture with the eye. Not even with the mind; not properly. I'd never been affected like that before Ceylon.

I hadn't thought of it much since, and certainly not in those ways—until I encountered the mystery of Queenie. How could she have woken all that up? But somehow she had, and I wanted to try and find a way to talk with her about it.

A month went by, and half of another. It was coming up to Christmas. The midwinter nights started in the middle of the afternoon, and in the mornings it didn't get light at all if there was any cloud cover. If there was a rare sunny day it would be almost noon before the tiny scatterings of garnet and quartz would sparkle and shine on the granite walls of the buildings of old Aberdeen.

Mr. B was indisposed all one weekend and I had to run the theatre. The lady from Bridge of Don was there to take care of the ticket booth, and the Greek girl had come in to run the concession stand. Beyond them, and two usherettes to show patrons to their seats, I was going to be on my own. It would make for a long Saturday. Looking back, though, I didn't really expect it to be much different from normal. Mr. B could get into the whisky on a Friday night, and sometimes on Saturdays as well, so I'd often wind up dealing with everything anyway—the staff, the reconciliations of the cash with the box office ticket numbers, the concessions and cash, the bank deposit, and so on. It was the Kid's Klub I was nervous about. When he was well Mr. B did the Kid's Klub on Saturday mornings, and he was good at it. The kids liked him, and he seemed to like them. On stage he was a natural. He made them laugh, and they loved the little tasks and tricks he got them to do. But when the kids saw me going up on the stage I'd see the disappointment on their upturned faces, sometimes even hear what sounded like a groan.

This particular Saturday, Queenie telephoned to say she would come in at lunchtime to give me a hand. She'd be happy, she said, to stay until closing if it would be helpful. It was up to me. I was glad of it. It took a weight off my mind. She was much better than I was at the reconciliations; better at the arithmetic. In fact she was better at everything an Assistant Manager had to do; better even than Mr. B. She did most of what he was supposed to do anyway.

She looked more pale than usual when she came in, just before noon on the Saturday morning. She was a bit earlier than I thought she'd be. I had been at the theatre since half past eight for the Kid's Klub, and the kids had not long left. I asked Queenie if she was all right.

"Yes," she said, "but I wonder if I could ask you to walk me back to my flat after we finish up tonight."

"Of course," I said. "Is there some difficulty?" Then I realised she'd be walking home about the time the pubs closed. I'd never thought of it before; not once in all those dark winter Saturdays; a single woman walking home about closing time, and not far from the docks either. It could be especially difficult if a team like the Glasgow Rangers had been playing at Pittodrie. Rangers' supporters had a reputation for doing more damage than anyone.

"There was an assault in the stairwell last night," Queenie said. "Someone followed a man who lives in the first floor flat and beat him up in the stair. He had to be taken to hospital."

"Gosh," I said. "That's terrible. I can phone up a couple of friends if you like. I'm sure they would come along with us. They play rugby for the university team. They're quite big."

Ally and Big John would often turn up at the theatre as we were closing on a Saturday night. They'd get me to take them over to the Palais dance hall behind the cinema. It was owned by the same company I worked for, and because of that I could get in free. I knew the bouncers on the door at the Palais, and they'd usually let me bring in a friend or two without them having to pay the entry charge. The bar at the Palais stayed open well past the closing time for the pubs, which made it attractive to my rugby playing pals.

Queenie smiled. "Oh, I think it will be all right. The police made an arrest. I don't think there will be any trouble. It's just . . . if you can accompany me I'll feel a bit safer."

As it turned out, Big John and Ally didn't come to the cinema that night. I walked Queenie down Union Street to the Mercat Cross and up to the door of her flat in Castle Street. I had half a mind to go back to the Palais myself. There was a girl who worked there I fancied, and it wasn't far out of my way back to Rosemount.

"Would you like to come up for a drink before you go home?"

I heard myself say "Yes", and it was done. I followed Queenie up the stairs to the black door.

"What would you like?" she said, when I was sitting in her living room. "I've got some whisky and some wine, and two bottles of Tennent's lager." She waited while I thought about it.

"The lager would be fine," I said. "Lovely in fact."

Queenie poured lager into one of those dimpled mugs you get in the pubs. I expected her to pour herself a glass of whisky, but she didn't. She came back from the kitchen with a glass filled with a white liquid.

"Gosh, that looks interesting," I said. "What is it?"

"Milk." She sat down on the couch, opposite me, on the other side of the electric fire. She gazed at the fire. It was one of those ones with little artificial flames that dance above the electric bars.

There was a long silence. I didn't know what to say. I'm not good at small talk; the weather, work, Aberdeen, and I could tell she wanted to say something.

"I was rude to you when you came to dinner," Queenie said.

"Pardon?" It wasn't possible. She'd cooked me a lovely meal and she'd been most kind.

"You asked me what I was doing in Ceylon, and I cut you off," she said. "I'm sorry."

"I'd love to hear about it if you'd like to tell me."

She didn't look at me when she spoke; just at the electric fire, and those artificial flames.

"They turned the racecourse at Colombo into an airfield," she said. "It's where I worked. I was with a special operations group there during the war."

My father was keen on the horse racing. He'd pointed the racecourse out to me one day when we were driving past it.

"Oh my," I said. "My father showed it to me. I remember the grandstand; a lovely big white building that looked as if it was made out of marble. I don't think they still had races there though." Queenie was gazing at the fire, going over memories I supposed. "Special operations sounds exciting. It must have been much more interesting than working here in Aberdeen. What were you doing?"

She didn't say anything for what seemed like a long time. It was an awkward silence, as if she wanted to tell me things, and yet not tell me. I took a sip of the lager, trying to think how I could make it easier for her—despite the fact the war was a long time ago, and I didn't actually think that working as a secretary or whatever she'd been at an airfield would have been all that interesting.

"I can't say much about it," she said. "We weren't allowed to talk about it. Basically our job was to send people into Malaya; sometimes up to Burma. The Japanese had invaded those countries. The people I worked with were sent behind the lines, to disrupt communications. Blow things up sometimes. That kind of thing. I was only a few years older than you are now."

"How did you get to do something like that?" I said.

"My job was to listen in to radio communications. I picked up messages from our people in the field; sometimes from the other side. The Japanese."

She hadn't answered my question, but I thought she would. She did, right away.

"Then I had to help prepare the people who would go in," she said, and her voice took a little jump; a little hiccup. "I could speak Japanese, and one of the native languages as well."

Thinking of the ἰχθύς and her pronunciation of the word, she probably spoke some Greek too. There was a lot more to Queenie than the people in Edinburgh had told me.

She began to speak about one of the men she'd worked with. What she said unwound gradually, until it took on a kind of intimacy that seemed extraordinary to me. Not so much because of what she told me—although it was surprising in the context of our day-to-day working environment—but because of the confidence she gave to me. All through the months I had known her I'd hardly known her at all—except as a quiet, reserved person who protected her privacy. What was unexpected was I could tell right away by how she spoke, by the cadences in her voice, that this person had been special to her. And young, yes. I could tell that from the way she spoke of him, from the words she used to describe him. And then, all of a sudden it was as if she knew she had said too much; gone too far.

Queenie stood up and looked down at the table; at the empty glasses, at me. It was like she'd woken up from a sleep. She half turned and reached for the door of the drinks cabinet behind her chair, seemed to collect herself, and asked if I would like the other bottle of lager. She had already opened the door of the cabinet, so I could tell she wanted to pour herself something stronger than the milk. The lager was in the small refrigerator in her kitchenette.

"If you're having one, I'll join you," I said.

She went through to get the lager for me, and came back and took a bottle of Buchanan's Black and White from the cabinet and poured some of it into her glass. It was the same kind of whisky Mr. B kept in his desk at the office.

"What was his name," I said. I knew it was all right to ask her about it; knew she wanted to talk about it; wanted to tell someone. Wanted to tell me, although I couldn't see why.

She didn't answer my question; not properly. "They called him Cav. It means 'poet' in Sanskrit."

I nodded. "Was he a poet?"

"In Tamil it's Kavi. But his proper name was Maari." Queenie moved in her chair.

I knew then that this conversation could never go outside the room of her small flat on Castle Street. Not to the office. Not anywhere. It would not be continued either. After this evening it would not have occurred. I knew that. Soon I was taking it in, all of it. Every word she said, and gradually, as I listened to Queenie's story, it was as if I could smell the sweet jasmine in my father's garden, the sandalwood on my shirts.

"Cav was Tamil, but he was also a Sikh."

I remembered a little bit about the Sikhs from the time I'd been in Ceylon. M'habbia had told me that they were actually a peaceful people, despite the fearsome reputation they had when they fought. He'd said that I could be a Sikh if I wanted; anyone could. I asked him if that would mean I'd have to wear a turban and carry one of these wonderful, curved knives. I was only eleven years old then and I liked the idea of it. Now I know the knife is called a Kirpan.

"We don't believe in cutting hair," was all M'habbia had said. "You wouldn't have to shave either." I hadn't started to shave by then. M'habbia knew I wasn't being serious, and he had the house to run.

"Did Cav have long hair?"

Queenie nodded. "He kept it wrapped in a turban most of the time. But at his house he would take the turban off and I would see his long, beautiful hair."

A tear ran down her cheek. She didn't try to stop it, she just looked away. Queenie, the tough woman I had been warned about. I was astonished.

She composed herself and turned back. It was only a minute. Less.

"It shone," she said. "It was the loveliest hair I have ever seen. Soft, but strong." She looked from the fire, up to my face.

Perhaps I showed surprise. She'd given me a shock. The intimacy of it. She must have been in Cav's house then, touched his hair, run her fingers through it. The conversation had taken a turn I hadn't expected. I wasn't sure what to say.

After a minute I said, "What does it mean? Maari?" I knew that names there often had special meanings.

"It's the name of a God," she said. "A name for God; but perhaps I didn't understand it well. It means 'rain' too. Rain from the sky; rain from tears. Cleansing rain. I should know. I cried when I knew I would never see him again. I weep for him now. Often. He was a beautiful man."

I looked at Queenie. It was as if I hadn't seen her before at all. And as I looked at her it seemed as if the years peeled away and I saw the young woman who had been in love with the Tamil Sikh. I saw more than that. I saw them on a warm night on the beach at Bentota. Perhaps on many warm nights.

Queenie was giving me a funny look. Not an angry look or anything like that. It's hard to describe what sort of look it was. It was more like a question.

"We were lovers," she said. Just like that, she explained the look. The question had been one for herself; if she should tell me or not. But I knew already, and I didn't know where to look, what to say. I was nineteen. I hadn't ever been with a girl or a woman, and in that moment I realised Cav was dead.

She stood up slowly. She was going to ask me something. Suddenly I was nervous; tingling in my stomach; butterflies. But she didn't say anything for what seemed like minutes; just looked down at the table, then at me.

"Can I show you something he wrote?" she said. "A poem."

"Yes, of course. I'd love to see it."

Queenie went through to what must have been her bedroom. I heard a drawer open and close, then her footsteps coming back down the hallway, click-click-click on the linoleum floor.

She put a piece of torn notepaper in front of me. Grey paper, folded. It had been torn in half, and half again at one time, and then patched together with what was now old, brittle sellotape. I opened it up carefully and laid it flat on the table in front of me.

Send me your eyes at the borderline
watching, wise.
Keep me safe when I fall.
Dark eyes, lined with life.
I love you so.

I looked up to her face and it seemed I saw her eyes as they had been, as he had seen them. "He wrote it for you?" I whispered. "It's beautiful."

There was a word scribbled in the margin in faded pencil at the end of the first line. '*Sadhana*', and just below it was that little symbol I'd seen on Queenie's wrist. It wasn't her writing.

Sadhana was a Hindu word. I knew the word; I had once asked my father what it meant. It had been written on a small sign at the airport at Colombo, in English, and also in the Hindi *nāgarī* and Tamil *vaṭṭeḻuttu* scripts. My father hadn't known what it meant. He'd told me to ask M'habbia when we got home.

M'Habbia had looked at me with a frown on his face. He asked me where I'd seen it. I told him, and he thought for a long moment before he spoke. *Sadhana* was a complicated word, he said. It could have lots of meanings. He himself had never been to the airport; never been on an aeroplane; never wanted to fly up in the sky. He didn't like the idea of it. It wasn't natural. He thought many Sri Lankan people would feel the same. Perhaps *sadhana* would be written on a sign at the airport to give faith to travellers who were afraid of flying.

I might also see it, he added, if I ever became a Sikh and went to worship at the Sri Guru Nanak Darbar at the Gurdwara in Sarasavi Lane in Colombo.

I tried to remember how M'Habbia had explained its meaning to me, a non-believer I suppose, and only a child then. It meant something about a transition, he explained, but it suggested opportunity; a difficult journey undertaken with hope. I didn't know what to say to Queenie, so I didn't say anything.

"Cav spoke Hindi and Tamil," she said. "We sent him to Perak on the coast of Malaya. There was a Sikh population there, and he would be able to absorb himself in it." There were no tears on Queenie's face now.

"Sometimes I would see the agents off at the airfield. But Perak was too far from Colombo for any of the aircraft we were able to fly from the racecourse. Cav was to go from the RAF base at Minneriya on a Liberator, a bigger plane with more range. The runway at Minneriya was almost a mile and a half long.

"It was a long journey across the island to Minneriya. It's about three quarters of the way to the navy base at Trincomalee on the east coast. A hundred and thirty miles or so, and the roads were not very good. We left Colombo two days before Cav was due to fly out in case there were delays. It was the time of the southwest monsoon, and sometimes there would be washouts. But the weather was quite stable as it turned out, and we made good time.

"We didn't say much to each other that day. Cav was a deeply religious man, and he had a lot to think about. I didn't want to get in the way of his thoughts." Queenie paused. "We were driving up the main trunk road. It's called the A6 now. Not long after we passed a town called Dambula, Cav asked me if I would take him to Sigiriya. I hadn't heard of it, but he said it was an important place, and it wasn't far off our route to the airfield at Minneriya."

It was as if Queenie had discovered a new kind of energy. Sustenance, perhaps, of a different kind, although maybe it was just the Black and White. Who knows, but she had all my attention that evening.

"Sigiriya is an enormous rock that climbs out of the forest. More than a thousand years ago a king built a palace up there. Part of the way up the climb you have to enter a cleft in the rock, and it's there that you pass through a gate they call the Lion Gate.

"We climbed up more than a thousand steps," she said, "and when we reached the top we entered a garden; a natural garden that had once been worked and farmed, and we thought of the silent monks who had lived through centuries when there was a monastery there. And I saw Cav's spirituality as a visible thing, like a light.

"Cav told me that Sigiriya was the city of the Gods, and in that moment he was Maari, and he looked at me in a way that nobody else ever has. 'You can feel it too,' he said. 'It is like a shining, a light, but it is not visible to those who do not share it. It is how I know.'

"I knew it because it was unlike anything I'd ever felt before, or anything I have felt in my life since that day," Queenie said. "Cav had been to Sigiriya before. It was where he got strength in difficult times. He told me of the caves where monks had lived a thousand years before, and of erotic frescoes they had left on the walls.

"I asked him to show the paintings to me," Queenie said. "It was difficult to get to them, and dangerous, but we climbed down by clefts in the rock to an ancient pathway that took us to one of the caves. The frescoes were beautiful. 'They are not of this earth,' Cav said. 'They are sky maidens.'"

I had never been with a woman then, and when Queenie, this old lady, began to speak about erotic frescoes I began to feel uncomfortable. I wanted her to stop. But she didn't.

Queenie took a sip of whisky, and went on. "I had never seen anything like the young women in those caves; never even imagined anything like them. Their bodies were exquisite, lithe and sexual. Ethereal. Then Cavi told me that I was one with them; that they would always make him think of me.

"There was no one else on the rock at Sigiriya that day," Queenie said. "For a few hours it was there just for us."

I knew she was going to say more, and I desperately wanted to change the conversation before Queenie went too far down the erotic track. That kind of intimacy would be all right now, but on that evening in Aberdeen it was uncomfortable.

"How could they have had gardens up on top of a rock? Gardens need water," I said. "Surely they can't have had water hundreds of feet up a rock."

"Oh yes," Queenie said. "The ancients had devised a system for getting water from pools in the forest up several hundred feet to the gardens and the farm plantings on the plateau. It was sophisticated; a kind of hydraulic system. They could get as much water as they wanted. On the day Cav and I were at Sigiriya, there were ponds on the plateau. Catchment basins for the monsoon rains." She smiled. "They were not modern constructions. No one has lived up there for centuries."

The smile left and the look on her face changed to no expression at all, an emptiness. It was sudden. Impossible to describe.

"I told you there was a Sikh population in Perak," Queenie said, "But most of the people there were Tamil. Cav handed me a pair of scissors and asked me to cut his hair. I hadn't known he was to go to Perak as a Tamil. I had thought he was to go as himself, as a Sikh; that it was why he had been selected for the operation. I should have known. Tamil is the predominant language; it's a larger component of the population than the Sikh.

"We sat up on Sigiriya and I cut his hair; his long, beautiful hair. He knew then he wouldn't come back," she said. "I knew too."

It seemed as if she was going to say something else, but no words came. Slowly, she pulled back the sleeve of her blouse to reveal the little tattoo I had seen before; the little ἰχθύς symbol under the word *sadhana* on that scrap of paper.

"We buried his hair at Sigiriya," she said.

I didn't ask her what had happened to Cav. I couldn't. Besides, Queenie had told me a lot; the parts that were important. I don't know if she had ever told anyone else, and there were things that could not be said. But I knew that hair for a Sikh had the most profound spiritual importance. *Kesh*, M'habbia had called it the day he'd told me I could become a Sikh if I wanted to.

"They sent me home from Ceylon several months later," she said. "I never saw Cav again." A tear ran down her cheek but she paid it no attention. Then another came and she turned her head. I didn't see her wipe the tears away. When she turned back her eyes were damp, but her cheek was dry.

"I was going to have his baby," she said.

There was no wedding ring. I didn't think Queenie had ever married. It would not have done then to have a child and not a husband. Besides, I knew it wasn't allowed in the forces in wartime.

"She was born a month after I got back to England," Queenie said. "It was a long journey by sea—round South Africa, up to Canada, and then across to Liverpool. When I got to England the war in Europe was over." She took a deep breath. "But the war with Japan was still going on; it went on until August that year."

I was already thinking about Queenie's daughter. She would be about the same age as me. I wondered what had happened to her.

"I had hope for years," Queenie said, "but I'd known at Sigiriya he wouldn't come back. When I cut his hair I took his power."

I must have looked sad.

"It's life," said Queenie. "What happened to Cav was life; what life was then anyway. Orders. You don't get choices in a war. It's all to do with circumstance and calculation. The circumstances were, well, what they were . . . and the people I worked with made the calculations. One for one. Sending Cav to Perak saved a life, and they paid for it with his."

Four floors below Queenie's flat the stair door slammed. Queenie jumped as if a shot had gone off. A splash of whisky went on the rug in front of the fire. A snatch of inebriated song echoed up the stairwell. "*I belong tae Glasgow. . .*"

Queenie looked at me and smiled. "It was Mr. B who arranged for me to go back to Britain. I didn't want to leave Ceylon, but there was no choice."

"Mr. B?" I said.

Queenie nodded. "Mr. B was the station chief in Colombo. Force one-three-six it was called. It was Mr. B who detailed Cav for the mission into Perak. He had to really. They needed to get someone out of Malaya, and they had a fishing boat to transport him. But they needed to put someone else in the field. A replacement who would fit in with the population. That was the dangerous part."

Her voice was crisp, and in the explaining she showed me what an efficient, dispassionate intelligence agent she would have been. What happened to Cav would have seemed like a good solution to the people at Force 136. Perhaps it was the only option available to them. Cav was Tamil; the other man was English. The English were not difficult to spot in Malaya. A Tamil agent could sink into the general population, and Perak had a Sikh minority as well. Cav was well-fitted for the role he had to play.

The Englishman got away and Cav was taken. Queenie thought it must have been soon after he arrived. She told me she didn't know what had happened. Mr. B didn't either, she said. Cav just disappeared. Returned to dust. No known burial. Queenie spoke of it in an empty voice. It was as good an example of acceptance as I was ever to see.

I began to understand that this was the only way Queenie could speak of that part of her life; through something of a philosophical dialogue. I also saw that it would have been Mr. B, as the head of operations at force one-three-six, who had made the decision about the Tamil rather than the Sikh. I wondered if he'd known what it would mean to Cav, or to Queenie.

I fancied a scent of sandalwood. I'm not sure why. Queenie was looking at me; all the way into me, and it seemed as if the years rolled away and I saw a young, twenty-two-year-old girl with a wonderful mind, and an ethereal beauty. What was she doing here, in this cold flat, working with a semi-alcoholic manager in a god-forsaken cinema in Aberdeen? And then I knew it was because poor old Mr. B was the only connection in the whole world to the love of Queenie's life, and to her loss.

"Five minutes with Cav," she said, "was worth every minute of my life."

It was my turn to weep. I didn't, but it felt like it inside.

"Why me?" I said, and she knew what the question was; knew what I meant.

"You remind me of him," she said. "I don't know why."

I never learned as much from anyone else as I did that evening.

I wanted to ask Queenie about her child, but I didn't know how to. It was too private, too intrusive. But I had a thought about that poster I'd seen the day I was looking for a pencil in her desk.

"Have you been back there, to Ceylon?" I said. "I mean, since your time there during the war?"

Queenie looked up. "Yes," she said. "I went there three years after the war ended. I took Mairi with me."

"Mairi?"

"Our child."

"Mairi," I said. "It's a lovely name." I had an aunt with the same name. She lived in Caithness, as far north as you can go on Scotland's mainland.

"I gave her the name because of her father, and because she was born out of love," Queenie said.

It was as close as it could be to Cav's given name. Maari, she had said.

"Why did you go back to Ceylon?"

"I wanted to take Mairi to Cav's sister. She would have brought her up as her own. But in the end I couldn't do that." Queenie gave me a look which went right through to my core. "I wanted to take her to the places that Cav and I had been to; to grow in the places where we'd made love, and the special place where she had come from."

The conversation had become so intimate that I told her about the thing that had been worrying me for so many weeks. I told her I'd been looking for a pencil and had gone to her desk to see if I could find one, and in doing that had come across the Ceylon poster. Queenie didn't seem concerned about it. Not even when I asked her about the pencilled lines on the back of the poster. I quoted them to her:

"*I am become life, creator of worlds.*" I asked her about the initials BG, and the question mark beside them.

She smiled. I liked her smiles. I had not expected them when I'd left Edinburgh to come north.

"It was something Cav said to me the evening we spent at the Lion Rock at Sigiriya. He said it to ease my anguish when I had to cut his hair. It's a change—a parody if you like—from the words in the Bhagavad Gita. BG." She smiled once more. "Some Sikhs think the Bhagavad is a poem from God." She looked away, at the dancing flames of her fire. "Sometimes I hear its music."

So, what did I learn? I saw Queenie as she had been—young, with the years pushed away—and yet not. I learned that old people are not so old; that they can show us they were once young, and remind us of that youth without explanation, without *telling* us. I learned how to see a depth of beauty in old people; a depth of beauty that's not available to the young.

It was a revelation; a light turned on.

There was much left unresolved when it came to Queenie. I never did find out what became of her child. She would have told me if she'd wanted me to know. And she never did say who had written those words on the back of the old BOAC poster. It was published in the 1950's, long after the events she had told me about.

"*I am become life, creator of worlds.*"

Deux Chevaux

The final class at the Université Libre in Brussels finished on the stroke of four o'clock. It was only a short, four-week course, but it had been intense. The Albigensian Crusade; the Papacy battling the Cathars for all of twenty years. I'd had enough of studies. That last class was a blank in my brain. I'd spent half of it looking out the classroom window, watching a girl circling the running track. There had been something mesmeric about the way her hair floated behind her as she ran, and her feet kicked up little clumps of red dirt. Some boys had been playing a pick-up soccer game on the grass field inside the running track. They were skilful, trapping the ball, passing it off, running for the return pass, energy in their movements. The girl had come round the track again, and again; elegance and grace. Beyond them grey buildings rose box-like on the other side of the playing field. There were young leaves on the trees.

The girl left the track and I focused on the class for a while. Through the window glass I could hear the boys kicking the ball around, but that runner had captured something in me. Then I saw that she had not gone after all. She was sitting at the side of the track, rubbing her feet, her shoes on the grass beside her. Someone scored a goal in the soccer game.

The girl stood up and walked across the field. Straight-backed, she walked right through the middle of the soccer game. She was barefoot, carrying her running shoes, one in each hand. The soccer game stopped, the boys waiting for her to cross; all of them watching her; the ball forgotten. I turned away from the window, back to the Albigensians and Pope Innocent, who was anything but.

At four o'clock it was time to leave Brussels. The rest of the summer stretched out with unquantifiable promise. I said goodbye to the others, and shook hands with one of them as we left the building. Jean-Pierre and I had sat side by side in the same hot classroom for the last four weeks.

"It has been good," I said. "Perhaps we will meet up again some day."

Jean-Pierre put his hand on my shoulder. "Where will you go now?" he said.

"I'm going to Edinburgh to see my mother," I said. "And you?"

"To the airport. My flight leaves at eight o'clock."

"To?"

"Montreal. I've been long enough in Europe. You were here for four weeks. I've been here for four years. It's time for me to go home."

"I've never been to Montreal," I said. "Perhaps I'll come and look you up one of these days. In the meantime I'll come with you to the airport and see if I can get a flight up to Edinburgh."

"You can't," said Jean-Pierre. "Not direct anyway. You will have to change flights somewhere—Gatwick or Stanstead I think. I tried to go to Edinburgh last year for the festival. It was expensive. Have you got enough money?"

"How much is it?" I said.

"Last year the flight cost about three hundred euros."

"Jeez," I said. "I've got exactly two hundred and eighty euros left."

We passed through the barrier at the main entrance to the university. My head was spinning. I could hitch-hike to the ferry at Ostend, but hitching these days was a drag. No one ever stopped to pick you up. I didn't fancy sleeping in a field halfway to the coast, with no tent and no sleeping bag.

There, right in front of us on the Avenue Franklin Roosevelt, a young fellow was sitting on the fender of an old Citroen. He was holding a sign: *'Deux Chevaux – US $100'* it read. It was a cute little car. Rugged in spite of its looks. I knew farmers used them.

The thing was, the little car was parked on the grass boulevard between the north and southbound lanes of the broad avenue. Rush hour traffic was whizzing by on either side. As we watched, a policeman drove up on a big BMW motorbike. The gendarme stopped and climbed off his bike.

"That will do me fine," I said to Jean-Pierre. I gave him a wave and dashed across the road. The policeman had just started talking to the guy with the Deux Chevaux when I reached them.

The policeman was speaking in French, and the young man with the sign didn't understand any of it. "Sorry," I heard him say in what sounded like a Brooklyn accent. "I don't understand a word you're saying pal."

My French was passable. The Albigensian Crusade had been conducted in French. It was part of my medieval studies.

The policeman was saying that he was going to write up a charge; that it was illegal to sell a car here on the edge of the university precinct, and a huge offence to park it on the boulevard.

"It's all right, officer," I said in French. "He's just trying to be funny. He's actually waiting for me." I looked at the American. "Tell the police officer you're sorry," I said in English, "Say you're not serious about selling the car. You were just waiting for me, to give me a lift."

The American was about to say something contrary back to me. I gave him a wink the policeman couldn't see. "Go ahead," I said, "and things will be fine."

The young fellow turned to the policeman. "I'm terribly sorry, officer. I didn't mean to offend you or to break any laws. My friend is here and we will leave now."

I translated it into French.

The policeman looked me up and down. "Your French isn't bad," he said, in almost accent-less English. "That's more or less what he said. But next time you give advice to someone like this keep your voice down so I can't hear what you're saying. Oh, and that wink. It would be a good idea to make sure I can't see it in the motorbike's mirror next time."

"I'm sorry, officer," I said.

"Get out of here," said the gendarme. He pointed at the Deux

Chevaux, "and take that pile of shit with you."

We climbed into the Deux Chevaux, the American and me.

"What's wrong with the car?" I said when we were driving up the Avenue Franklin Roosevelt.

"Nothing. There's nothing wrong with it. You can do almost anything to this little number and it will still get you to wherever you're going."

I thought I was right about his accent. Well, almost. Closer up it sounded softer than Brooklyn. Perhaps Queens. He was about the same age as I was. "Where are you from?" I said.

"New Jersey," he said. "I've been on an exchange from Princeton and I'm flying out tomorrow. I've pretty well got to take what I can get for this little pigeon. I figured a hundred bucks was a fair deal."

He had an honest face so I said. "I'll give you a hundred euros for it. It's all I can manage."

"That's okay," he said. "As I say, I've pretty well got to take what I can get for it."

Later I realised that I'd paid him more than he'd asked for by about ten per cent, given the exchange rate. He hadn't corrected me—which was probably why he was a Princeton student and I wasn't. On the other hand I figured out when I managed to look up the ferry timetables and fares, that the cost of the car, the gasoline, and the ferry from Ostend to Dover would be cheaper than the air fare to Edinburgh by a long way. But, as I say, that was later.

He turned off Franklin Roosevelt onto a side street called the Avenue de l'Orée and parked. We got out of the little car.

"What about you," he said. "You're not from the States. Where are you from?" I liked that he didn't just hold out his hand for the money. Still, I hadn't brought out my wallet yet.

I didn't give him a direct answer. "I'm heading up to Edinburgh," I said. "I was going to catch a flight this evening." I walked round the little car. It was a grey colour with a roll-back, soft-top to it. There were a few dents in the bodywork.

Something struck me. "The regular term is still in session here.

How come you're going back to the States now?"

He looked at me and looked down at his shoes. His body listed a little to the left. He gazed down the street as if the answer would come walking towards him. "It's complicated," he said. "Some things didn't work out."

"That's a shame." I'd done a few overseas studies. "Schooling's different in different places. It's not always what we expect."

He looked away down the street again. A man and a woman came out of an apartment building and turned up the sidewalk towards us. They were holding hands.

"It's not that. It's a girl," he said, and his face had lost something—an energy, a sparkle from his eyes perhaps. For a moment he looked unutterably sad.

He gathered himself and patted the car, making a soft drum sound on the fabric of the roll-back roof with his fingers. "Ever driven one of these things before?" he said.

"Can't say I have."

"It's a real trip." He opened the door. It was small inside. The seats were made of a stiff canvas, held onto the frame with hooks and what looked like thick rubber bands. There was a big, yellow daisy on the metal dash; one of those stick-on, plastic things.

"Hop in," he said. "If you're really going to buy it we should take a drive round the block." He handed me the key and walked round to the passenger side.

We got in. I put the key in the slot and turned it. A light on the dash came on but nothing else happened. "How do you start it?" I said.

He pointed at a black button. "Just push that."

I pushed it and the engine coughed into life.

I looked down for the gear lever. There was nothing there.

"The gear shift is a bit weird," he said. "It's this thing sticking out of the dash." He patted a horizontal lever that curved upwards at its end. There was a big knob about the size of a tennis ball on the end of it. "First gear is immediately left when you pull the lever out. For second and third gears you just bring it back some more. To get fourth gear you turn the lever to the right when you're in third."

"Where's reverse?"

"Opposite first gear. Just turn the lever the other way"

"Weird is right," I said. "It's like something you'd see at the funfair."

"You'll get used to it. Fourth gear's got a flywheel that works like an overdrive," he said. "When you get on the highway it saves you a ton of gas. You just find the right level with the throttle pedal and it takes care of it. You'll soon get the hang of it."

"Anything else?" I wanted to get going. I might even get to Calais if I pushed it. The Calais-Dover ferry was cheaper than going from Ostend.

"It only goes about fifty," he said. "And the windshield wipers don't work when the car's stopped. They function with the speed of the car."

We went round the block. It was easy enough to drive when I'd figured out it operated to a different kind of logic than I was used to. Acceleration wasn't much to speak about, but once it got going everything seemed to work.

"It's fine," I said when we got back to Franklin Roosevelt. "I'm happy to go ahead with the deal."

I didn't have a hundred euros in cash. I had travellers cheques. I took two fifties from the folder. He looked doubtful. "They're travellers cheques," I said. "Legal tender."

"I've never seen a travellers check before," he said. "I just use my credit card when I'm travelling. Or dollars; everyone takes US dollars."

I pulled out my wallet and took out an American Express credit card. "If you can process this that's fine by me."

"No," he said. "I can't do that obviously. I'll take your word for it."

I handed the cheques to him; American Express, like my credit card. "You see my signature at the top corner? The way the banks work is you have to sign these things when you buy them. When you cash them you sign them here." I pointed. "So I need to sign them both to make them live." I signed the cheques. "Now you or anyone else can exchange them for cash at a bank, or you can use them for a purchase."

"You're sure that works?"

I nodded. "I guess this whole transaction is a trust thing," I said. "I'm trusting you when you say your car will get me to Edinburgh. You're trusting me that the money I'm giving you is kosher." I looked at him. "We could swap cards or contact addresses if it makes you feel better."

He shook his head. "Good luck with the Deux Chevaux. It will get you to where you're going, probably on one tank of gas. It hardly seems to burn the stuff."

"Good luck with the girl," I said. I don't know why I said the next thing, it just came out. "She's not a runner is she?"

I could see him in the rear view mirror as I drove away. He was staring at the retreating car, with his mouth open.

Transactions with the Fallen

Havock and spoil and ruin are my gain.
He ceas'd; and Satan staid not to reply,
But glad that now his Sea should find a shore . . .

John Milton, *Paradise Lost*, Book Two

The Piano Player

The boy shivered and pulled his coat tight. The wind was sharp, sweeping across the plain, dipping and swirling over the frozen ground, hugging the land, searching, biting. His eyes watered. He blinked and rubbed them. The cold burned the back of his throat, and froze the little hairs in his nostrils. It was so cold it was hard to breathe. He rubbed his nose with the back of his hand, and couldn't feel the coarse wool of his gloves.

He could make them out now, black figures on a white landscape; small, scattering, coming together, scattering again—like bees. There must be a thousand of them. He gripped his rifle and shrank into the hollow he'd blown in the frozen ground with a hand grenade.

He shook as he brought the rifle to his shoulder, teeth chattering, *chittety—chittety—chittety*. He was frightened. There were more of them now, running. More. A hundred, a thousand, more, and horses, galloping, stumbling, swerving, slipping.

The guns started up and the ground staggered as clods of iron earth fell like rain, bruising his back, his shoulders and legs—as if the sky was falling. The noise of it; explosions, screaming shells, whistling shrapnel, and an age later, the thud-thud-thud of frozen earth hammering the frozen ground.

Pillars of smoke rose to the sky, red-tinged at their roots. His guns were firing behind him now. The figures on the plain swerved apart, and came together; running, jumping, falling down. Horses, with white breath streaming from their nostrils, eyes wide with fear, steam spinning from their flanks, grey lather spraying from their necks.

A tear ran down his cheek, and froze. Beneath the coat he'd taken from dead Hansi, under two pairs of battledress trousers it was warm where he'd wet himself. Guns were firing everywhere now; the deep bark of 88's firing flat across the plain, and the rhythmic chatter of machine guns. And still the Russians came. On and on. Shells coming in, whistling like . . .

When Joachen awoke, he was lying against a low stone wall; drifted snow by his face. His eyelids were stuck together. He shook his head. Coloured lights flashed behind his eyeballs. Pain shot sharp through his head and shrank his scalp. He gasped.

A Russian soldier was watching him; black eyes set in a broad face; fur cap with leather flaps over his ears. His green-brown coat bulged like a barrel from his shoulders, held closed by bandoliers of ammunition. The soldier swayed, leaned into the wind, and knocked one boot against the other, the black snout of a sub machine gun cradled on his forearm.

Joachen raised himself on an elbow, and turned his head. Three of his companions sat against the wall. Red-eyed, with stubbled faces. Mueller the sergeant, Frans, and Hassen from the machine gun section. The Russian stamped his feet, one to the other and back. The muzzle of his gun moved from one of them to the other, never still for long.

Joachen lay for an hour as the Russian shifted his weight from one foot to the other foot, and said nothing. Beyond the Russian, the world was white. To his left, the broken roof beams of a stone farmhouse pointed fingers at low, leaded clouds. Mueller hummed softly to himself, his tune lost in the wind.

A door opened in the wall of the farmhouse and hung on a single hinge. Two soldiers tramped across the yard. They bent, and lifted Hassen to his feet and took him off to the farmhouse, stumbling, cursing at Hassen's unsteadiness. The door opened and Joachen heard a snatch of song. The door closed and there was only the wind, searching for gaps among the stones in the wall. Five minutes passed. There was a burst of shots, and a raven flew from a wrecked barn, black against the sky.

The two soldiers came from the farmhouse again, and summoned

Mueller to his feet. Mueller limped between them, blood dripping from his thigh. The soldiers opened the farmhouse door and a small shaft of light speared yellow at the dusk. More singing. The light went when the door closed, the song silenced. Minutes passed. There were more shots, and Mueller didn't come back.

They took Frans next. Frans, who had studied medicine at Dresden before the war; who was going to finish his degree and become a doctor when the war ended. Frans, who was gentle, who had tried to help Hansi when a plate-sized piece of shrapnel tore off his arm. Joachen felt his stomach tighten, and retched, and nothing came except for a dribble of spittle which froze before it reached the ground.

When they came for him, Joachen couldn't stand. The soldiers pulled him up by the collar of his coat. One of them poked the nose of a gun into Joachen's back and the other dragged him through the snow in Frans's footsteps, Hassen's sloughed furrows, and Mueller's blood-tinged tracks.

The soldiers threw the door open and pushed Joachen along a stone-flagged hallway lit dimly by the throw of light from oil lamps in the room at its end. Joachen heard the clink of glasses, and a bottle smash against stone. Shards of glass skittered across the floor, twinkling and flashing as they caught the light.

He was thrust into a room with half a ceiling, ragged plaster on the walls, and a floor littered with rubble and broken tiles. Six soldiers were standing around an old piano. Three more were sitting at a wooden table, and two on top of a big, brass casket. Another was asleep in a corner, knees drawn up, snoring, a medal ribbon on his chest. The soldiers dragged Joachen to the group at the piano.

"Namen?" one of them said in German, his eyes unfocused, his lips wind-chapped and red.

Joachen reached at the piano to steady himself.

"Joachen Lieb," he said, and his voice sounded to him as if it was coming from a deep tunnel.

"Regiment?" The Russian lifted a glass of clear liquid, flung his head back and swallowed. He belched, and wiped his mouth with the back of his hand. The others watched.

"18th SS Panzergrenadier."

The Russian stretched his arm out, the glass in his hand, his eyes on Joachen. A soldier poured more of the colourless liquid into the glass. The officer drank and threw the glass away, and reached out suddenly and grabbed Joachen's wrist, and peeled back his glove. The wool came away from Joachen's grey skin, ingrained along its lines and down its pores, with dirt.

Joachen couldn't stop shaking. The Russian turned the wrist over and examined the palm of Joachen's hand. He gestured at the battered piano.

"Spielen klavier?" he said.

Joachen gasped, opened his mouth and nodded. The Russian clapped him on the back, and turned to his comrades. The others moved aside. The men at the table stood up, moved forward, and half-carried Joachen to a chair. They picked up the chair with Joachen in it, and carried him to the piano.

"Spielen!" said the officer. He waved the soldiers aside, and they shuffled back to make room for the pianist.

Joachen ran his fingers soundlessly up and down the keyboard, touching it without pressure. He let his fingers rest on the keys for a long moment. Then he began to play, softly, feeling his way, coaxing the piano's battered insides. The old piano began gently to respond. Joachen played Rachmaninoff, the flowing power of the steppes. While he played the soldiers moved imperceptibly, instinctively closer to the piano. When he finished, the Russians applauded, and Joachen smiled at the circle of faces.

One of the soldiers was leaning on the back of the piano, black hair, a smile on his planed features, his eyes glazed. He handed Joachen a glass of clear slivovitsa. Joachen sipped it. The liquor bit the inside of his mouth, burned down his throat, and expelled the air from his lungs. He sneezed. The soldiers laughed. Joachen's stomach grew warm. He felt hope.

The officer stepped forward and the soldiers backed away to make space for him. He put a hand on Joachen's shoulder. His front teeth were broken. "As long as you play you will live," he said. "When you stop we will shoot you."

Joachen felt his face pulling. His knees shook. He gripped the side of the chair to stop shaking; to stop himself sinking into a bottomless place.

He played Liszt, the Hungarian Rhapsodies. One of the soldiers dropped to his haunches and kicked out his legs in a burst of energy. Two more stepped off in a fury of movement, whirling each other on bent arms, shouting as Joachen played. Another put a glass of vodka on top of the piano, and someone pushed a thick, lit cigarette between Joachen's lips. Smoke curled into his eyes, and he began to cough. He spat the cigarette out, and played on, the world withering to the black and white keys under his fingers.

The Russians remained at the piano when he finished the Liszt, smiles dissipating slowly. Artillery rumbled in the deep background. Joachen was tired. It was hours since he'd slept, longer since he'd tasted anything other than potatoes, or turnips, or the heavy *kammisbrot*. The officer cracked his glass on top of the piano, spilling vodka.

"Spielen!" he said. Joachen moved his fingers across the keys, forcing himself to concentrate. He stretched his fingers, and began to caress the notes from a Chopin nocturne. The soldiers smiled. He was reaching them. They wanted him to play; wanted him to stay alive.

The nocturne finished. One of the Russians pulled a creased photograph from his pocket; a picture of a young woman holding a little girl; the child smiling, the woman pretty, a scarf with white dots on her head.

"Mien frau," said the Russian. "Meine liebe."

Joachen swallowed. "I hope you can see them soon," he said.

Another soldier rested his chin on the back of the piano, absorbing the notes, consuming them, his eyes on the piano player. Joachen began to play folk songs from the forest country in Bohemia; songs he had learned from his grandmother in Haidmühle; soft, mystical music.

The Russians were all around the piano now, swaying as Joachen played, moved by the music. Joachen felt hope again. He couldn't help it.

A man in a brown-green uniform was sitting at a table in a corner of the bombed-out room, a thin, red armband on his sleeve. He wrote purposefully, the pencil moving slowly across the pages of his notebook. His eyes were heavy-lidded, and he had almost no neck. Every few seconds he put the tip of his pencil to his pink mouth, and his tongue stabbed at the lead like the flick of a snake's tongue.

"Commissar," whispered the soldier who had shown Joachen the photograph. "He watches."

Another glass was placed on the piano. "For you," said the officer. "Trinken!"

The vodka made Joachen dizzy. He shook his head to clear it. The officer laughed, slapped his thigh, and clapped Joachen on the back again. "A drink for men," he shouted. "Not for boys." The soldiers laughed.

"There are boys here too, in this war," said the man who had shown Joachen the photograph. The others stared at him.

"Ah, Andrej," said the officer. He shook his head. "Always the philosopher."

Joachen began to play again, this time with only his left hand; part of a piece Maurice Ravel had written for a friend, a concert pianist who had lost his right hand in the Austro-Prussian war. With a required finger span of twelve notes, Joachen had never learned to play it well. But now his hand spanned the keys, moving up and down the keyboard as if he had played it all his life.

The soldiers listened in silence, clapped when Joachen finished, and poured more vodka for this talent.

Joachen shook his head, his bones like weights, his muscles weak, his scalp contracting, the flesh hanging from the bones of his face.

The soldiers waited. Joachen smiled at the hazy faces above the piano. The faces smiled back. If he could keep playing until dawn the Russians would move on and he would be all right.

The Russian officer leaned in. "You must keep playing," he said, glancing at the commissar.

Joachen played a song from the Volga, and another; an emptiness in his stomach. Was it only a year since he'd heard that folk music in the little house on the outskirts of Rostov? A year; a lifetime of heat and cold, and fear. A year without sleep. A year with combat rations all the long way back to this ruined farmhouse in southeast Poland.

Some of the Russians were singing. This was music that could have come from Joachen's own childhood. The voices rose, dropped, and rose again. The Commissar looked up from his notebook, and frowned, licked his pencil, and bent again to his notes. Joachen coasted with the songs, with the soldiers. He swayed and banged out the beat of a Georgian drinking song. The soldiers clinked glasses.

The man who'd showed him the photograph held his glass to Joachen's mouth, and tilted it so that Joachen had to drink. Arms swung back and forth in front of him, back and forth. He began quietly to sob. His face twisted, his head dropped and his hands fell from the keyboard. The singing faltered, died away, stopped.

Joachen crashed his hands on the keys. Tried to play; tried to make sense of it, tried again. He was so tired. It was so long since he'd begun to play. The Russians had been drinking all the time. They didn't tire. He must keep on.

His mouth was dry, his tongue swollen, his head splitting and buzzing from the explosions and the confusion of vodka. His fingers would not answer his directions. Tears chased down his face.

The soldiers took his arms and helped him from the chair, half carrying him because his legs wouldn't work. They took him from the room, and he wept. The commissar, hunched over his notebook, did not lift his head.

They carried Joachen out into a wan, early dawn with pewter clouds skidding across a pale sky. The wind skewered through his clothes, carried away his breath, and froze his tears.

The soldiers propped him against the wall of the farmhouse, pushed his shoulders back so the cold stone would hold him. Joachen saw a bare, twisted tree, and an endless plain, white with snow. He saw a stubby machine gun swing on a short leather strap, waist high in front of a long, green coat; saw the flash from its muzzle; felt nothing. Nothing. Nothing.

Not even pain.

Inside the farmhouse the man who'd shown Joachen the photograph stuck his boot in the back of the piano and pushed it as hard as he could. It crashed onto the floor, splintered wood and jangled, severed strings. A black note flew from the keyboard and knocked the commissar's pencil, jarring the lead across the page. The commissar looked up and stared at the philosopher, frowned, dabbed his finger on his tongue, smudged it down on the page, and bent to his notes.

Transactions with the Fallen

Frankfurt. September 4, 1945—Tuesday
Staff Sergeant Linus Dumka shook his head. "I dunno where they find that stuff, but boy, they're good at it." He stared down at the top of Corporal Lester Concord's head. "Scavengers, Concord. Pros."

Concord grunted. He was writing in the inventory roster. It took concentration. His tongue worked its way carefully across his upper teeth and back again as he wrote.

Dumka moved to the window and looked down at the street. "Dunno how they do it. Goddam Polacks," he muttered, forgetting his own heritage.

"Don't know if they're really Polish, do we Sarge? Don't know who anyone is these days. Lotsa them claim to be who they're not."

The other side of the street was an unbroken mound of grey rubble with a thick growth of weeds and scrub bushes binding it together. Rosebay willow fronds swayed in the breeze that fanned the dusty ruins of what had once been a neat street of office buildings at the edge of Frankfurt's business district.

Dumka was still staring out of the window when Sauer walked out of the U.S. Army Ordnance Headquarters building for the Rhine-Main Military District several floors below. Bittner trudged after him, a step or two behind. Dumka watched them for a moment before turning back into the room on the fourth floor of the only building that was still useably intact within a half kilometre of the city's centre.

"How much've they made in the last week Concord?"

"I'll tell ya in a minute, Sarge," said Concord as he painstakingly added the figures on the page. He straightened up, chewing the end of his pencil. "I make it about twenty-two thousand marks. Since last Monday."

Dumka let out a slow, soft whistle. "Jeez." A flicker of doubt crossed his face. "Say Concord. How much is that?"

Concord was expecting the question. The Staff Sergeant was not strong on mental arithmetic. "About eight thousand bucks, Sarge." He scanned the page in front of him. "They've brought in four jeeps, a personnel carrier, a coupla dozen tents, eighteen combat jackets . . ." He stared at the paper ". . . thirty pairs of paratroop boots."

"Paratroop boots?" said Dumka. "Where in hell would they find paratroop boots? Our boys don't leave their boots lying around." He scratched the side of his nose. "Even if they did, everyone wants paratroop boots. The civilians would take 'em."

"Everyone's got paratroop boots these days, Sarge. Most of our army's in them now."

"Funny how they don't find weapons."

Concord thumbed through a pile of papers in front of him. "They do sometimes. About four weeks ago was the last time. They brought in some Panzerfaust and some Bazookas, and . . ." he flicked over the page ". . . some carbines. Not much though."

"Didn't they come up with a tank a while back?"

"Tank Destroyer. Told our boys where to find it anyway. They couldn't bring it in themselves. Their truck wasn't big enough. Said they found it in the forest up by the Belgian border."

"Twenty-two thousand marks," said Dumka. He looked at Concord. "Ain't much use to them is it? They can only spend marks in Germany and there ain't nuthin' to buy here."

Concord shrugged. "It's better than nothing, Sarge. That stuff works on the black market. And there's another thing; we printed that occupation money after we took over this place. They can change it at any U.S. Army post office for real dollars."

"They can't change it," said Dumka. "They're not in our army. It's not legal for Germans to have U.S. currency."

The door burst open as a dapper, chubby-faced officer strode into the room. Dumka snapped to attention. Concord jumped out of his chair.

"At ease!" Captain Miller gazed round the office. Files were stacked up on a table and on both desks. A pile of boxes lay untidily along a wall. "Don't you guys do any work in here? I said I wanted this place cleaned up."

"Yessir." Dumka stared rigidly at a spot on the wall above the Captain's head. He took a deep breath. "We've been kinda busy with all this surplus stuff coming in these last few days, sir."

"I saw those two guys going out the front door," said Miller. "Brought some more stuff in, did they?"

"Well, yes sir." Dumka drew himself up defensively. The Captain had asked questions about them before. It was obvious he didn't like them. He seemed to blame Dumka for dealing with them—even though it was his job to deal with them. "There have been others too, sir," Dumka went on. "There's a lot of materials lying around; all over the countryside, sir."

"I don't like Krauts," said the Captain.

"They're Polish, sir. Not German," said Dumka.

"Never heard him speak," said the Captain. "Not the tall one. The other one does all the talking."

"The tall one was shell-shocked, sir," said Dumka. "He got caught in a Russian artillery barrage while he was trying to escape. His wife and daughter were killed. Lost his farm and his house... everything."

"Doesn't speak, eh? That's what the other one told you?"

"Yessir."

Captain Miller nodded. "It's the tall one who's in charge," he said. "I can tell you that. Every time I've seen them the other one looks at him first before he says anything." He sniffed. "I don't like 'em. Don't trust them. Neither of them."

"No sir," agreed Dumka.

"Can't trust the Krauts. Can't trust goddam Polacks either."

"No sir."

"How much have we paid 'em since they started bringing in military equipment?" Miller turned quickly to face Concord. "Corporal?"

"I'm not sure how much in total, sir. It would take a while to work it out."

"Tomorrow then. I want the numbers tomorrow."

"I'll get them for you by then, sir."

"By oh-nine-hundred. Good." Miller nodded. Without saluting he turned and walked out. The door shut hard behind him.

They listened to the sound of Miller's boots receding down the corridor.

"Prick," said Dumka, but not too loudly.

Bittner steered the old Mercedes truck carefully through the eastern outskirts of the city. Frankfurt's suburbs rose up on either side of the road in mounds of rubble several metres high. They were not far from the old road to Hanau.

Sauer peered through the grimy windshield. "Up here," he said, pointing.

Bittner turned the truck onto a rutted track that weaved between more ruins. Gaunt and gutted buildings stood among piles of shattered bricks, mortar and dust. Charred roof beams pointed aimlessly skywards. Bittner drove slowly past a wall that was leaning dangerously close to the point of balance, waiting for the autumn winds to bring it down. Whitewash had been smeared across it in a vain attempt to hide some old lettering. *'Es liebe der Führer'*.

"Now, right," muttered Sauer.

"I know."

Sauer glanced at him, frowning. Bittner hauled on the wheel and eased the truck through a small gap in the ruins. He drove under a dark canvas covering beside a ruined house and switched off the engine. He jumped down from the cab, walked to the rear of the truck, and pulled down a tarpaulin to hide the truck from the outside.

Both men had been involved with Germany's wartime intelligence services. Sauer, a Berliner, had been an officer with the sinister Sicherheitsdienst, the intelligence arm of the SS. Bittner had been a junior officer with the Abwehr, Germany's regular military intelligence. He came from Orunia, near Danzig in East Prussia. The village had been part of Germany until East Prussia was overrun by the Russian Army in early 1945. Bittner spoke Polish and German. Survivors, both of them understood that chaos is an asset to people who wanted to cast off old identities. They had formed a doubtful partnership, and they had found cracks in the systems run by the victors.

A considerable amount of damaged and discarded military equipment was lying around the German countryside in 1945; American and German equipment. Tanks, trucks, jeeps and kubelwagens, usually damaged or burned out. They'd even found weapons like bazookas, panzerfaust, and rifles. The administration in the American occupation sector was trying to clear up as much military detritus as they could before it fell into the wrong hands, for some of it still worked. At the time it was widely believed that an underground force called *Werwolf* was going to keep on fighting.

Sauer and Bittner had scoured the countryside all summer, looking for equipment they could take into the Ordnance Depot in Frankfurt. The Americans paid well for it. At some point Sauer had discovered a U.S. Army department that was selling off surplus equipment—jeeps and tractors, boots and clothing, kitchen equipment, office equipment. It was military, but it wasn't weapons, and in a country where few people had any money, it was going cheap.

Sauer and Bittner had occasionally bought items of equipment from the Army surplus store, dirtied it up to look as if they had found it, and sold it to the Ordnance Deport in Frankfurt. It was the kind of thing that was happening in the chaos of nineteen forty-five.

The cellar of the ruined house they'd taken over was dry and undamaged. The walls were bare stone. A storm lantern hung on a short piece of chain from a beam. A stained grey carpet covered most of the floor. There were two cots, a small table and a pair of straight-backed wooden chairs. A petrol-fired primus stove sat on a shelf under some steps, and a paraffin lamp stood on a table. Boxes were stacked up to the ceiling in one corner of the room. Almost all of them were U.S. Army issue, with stencilled markings like 'Ration 10-1', 'Rations-WT 45 Menu 5', and 'US Army Field Ration K Supper Unit'.

Sauer pulled a chair up to the table and sat down. He took a small, dog-eared notebook from his pocket. Bittner unlaced his boots and lay back on one of the cots, his feet balanced on the rail at the end.

"Tomorrow will be our last transaction," said Sauer.

Bittner lifted his head. "Why? We're doing all right. This is the easiest way to make money I've ever seen."

Sauer put the book down. "That's the trouble with you, Bittner. You're greedy as well as stupid. You don't know when to stop and change direction."

He flicked through a few pages of the notebook. "The American Captain at the Ordnance Headquarters has begun to take an interest in us. He has watched us each of the last three times we have been there. He will ask questions about us. In a few days he will speak to his Major. Then the Major will speak to his Colonel."

Sauer's lip curled. "Then they will pick us up, Bittner, and they will question us. And you will probably tell them everything you know . . . and then we will be in a lot of trouble."

Bittner was sitting on the edge of the cot now, his hands on his knees. "How do you know this, Herr Sauer?"

Sauer slapped the palm of his hand on the table top.

Bittner swallowed, and wiped his hand across his mouth.

"Because I observe people and because I know the workings of the mind. Some of us made use of our training, Bittner." Sauer turned his attention back to the notebook.

After a few minutes he said, "We will go there late in the afternoon on Thursday; about the time they want to be finished for the day, so they will deal with us quickly. The next morning you will go and meet the man Walters from the U.S. Army post office, and arrange to change the rest of the money. You will offer to pay him the same commission as usual. You won't offer him more, even though this will be the last time. You don't want to make him suspicious."

"What if he wants more?" Walters had explored this possibility the last time.

"Then give in to him and leave as quickly as you can. But calmly, Bittner, calmly."

Bittner took a deep breath. He hated the shiftless meetings with Walters. They made him feel exposed and vulnerable.

"What will we do then?"

"I will tell you on Friday," said Sauer. "Don't worry, Bittner. I won't disappear. We Poles must stick together."

Frankfurt. September 7, 1945—Friday
Bittner lay on his cot, staring at the ceiling, watching the peeling, dirt-grey paint lighten as the dawn crept through the small, muddied window above his head. The silence was complete. There were no sounds even as the sky began slowly to show shades of grey. There was no singing of birds, no rumble of trains or traffic, no car horns, no human noise. In the great German cities, in the ruins of nineteen-forty-five, the silence was pervasive. When people spoke in the streets, they conversed in whispers. When children shouted at play their parents told them to be quiet. Nobody wanted to draw attention. It was as if people were afraid to waken the dead who still lay in the rubble.

Sauer was six feet away, lying on the other cot. Bittner could tell from his breathing that he was awake. He drifted with his thoughts for few minutes more.

"Breakfast, Bittner!" Sauer's dry voice pulled him back; back to this time, this place. Bittner sat up and swung his feet onto the stone floor. It was musty in the cellar, the air thick and close after days of warm, thundery weather.

Sauer was propped on one elbow, watching as Bittner fired up the primus stove and put a pan of water on to boil. Bittner moved to a cupboard in a corner of the cellar and opened the door. The cupboard was stacked with tins of spam and corned beef, and a few cans of vegetables and fruit. He reached in and took down two waterproofed cardboard boxes. The boxes were marked 'Breakfast' in clear black stencil. Smaller print on the side of each box indicated 'Field Ration K'.

Bittner opened the boxes and took a tin from each one. He picked up a bayonet from the table and punched a hole in each tin. He placed the two tins in the water that was already bubbling on the primus stove.

"Eggs, Bittner. I am hungry this morning." Sauer was sitting up in his cot. He waved his hand. "Eggs. Over by the door. I got them yesterday." He chuckled. "They cost me a packet of cigarettes. We must eat them while they are fresh." He stretched, and scratched under his arm. "I don't want those terrible dry crackers today either. I got some bread in exchange for a packet of coffee. It is over there too, wrapped in paper."

Bittner took a fruit bar from one of the boxes and offered it to Sauer. "It will keep you going while I cook the eggs," he said.

"No," said Sauer. "Open me a tin of real fruit. You can have one too if you want. It is good for you."

They ate their eggs in silence. Bittner tore a piece of bread from the loaf and used it to mop around the inside of his tin dish.

"You have no manners, Bittner," said Sauer. "Look at you. You will never get anywhere in life until you learn manners. You eat like a peasant. I find it irritating. You should close your mouth when you eat."

Bittner took another piece of bread and made an effort to keep his mouth closed while he chewed it. He swallowed, and took a packet of Nescafé from each box. He emptied the packets into tin mugs, and filled the mugs with boiling water from the kettle on the primus.

"How much money have we got now?" he asked as he sat down.

Sauer studied his coffee mug. "I don't know. I haven't counted it."

"Perhaps we should do that. Perhaps it is time for us to go in our own directions."

Sauer, the trained interrogator, knew that the tone in Bittner's voice indicated uncertainty. "No," he said. "Not yet my dear Stefan. Ah ... there is a lot for us to do yet. Many opportunities. Besides, we still have to change the marks we got from yesterday's business into hard dollars. You must make arrangements this morning with the man at the U.S. Post Office. What is his name?"

"Walters."

"Yes, Walters. You must meet him at the usual place; on his way to work."

Bittner considered this. "It was difficult the last time."

"I told you they were starting to get suspicious. You must be careful." Sauer's tone was conciliatory; agreeable.

"They didn't pay us what the equipment was worth yesterday," said Bittner.

"No. But if we had argued with them they might have done a check. Perhaps they have started one already." Sauer reached under his cot for his boots.

"What will we do afterwards then?" said Bittner. "You said you would tell me today."

"Opportunities, my dear Bittner. There are a lot of opportunities." Sauer tugged at the leather laces of his right boot. "I will tell you about them later. After you have changed the money." He looked up. "But I can tell you it will make us more money; much more."

Bittner was unconvinced. "Tell me now," he said.

Sauer straightened up. The lace of his left boot was partially tied. "Very well. I will tell you what I have planned. But first, some more coffee." He held out his mug.

Bittner opened another packet of Nescafé and poured hot water from the kettle. He handed the mug back to Sauer and waited.

"The black market," said Sauer. "I have been in touch with some people here in Hanau. They are running a big operation into the French zone."

Bittner listened. Everyone knew about the black market. It ran quite openly and there were enormous profits to be made. With the German economy in ruins most commerce worked on a barter system. All you had to do was find out which commodities were in short supply in different parts of the country. If you could acquire the things that were needed there were people who were ready to trade for them. Gold rings, antique furniture, family silver. Valuables like these could be swapped in some cities for food.

"What kinds of things are they selling?" asked Bittner.

"They are well organised," said Sauer. "Sometimes they use trucks, sometimes even trains. They bring food, soap and cigarettes up from the south, through the Frankfurt area and into the Ruhr. They return with cameras, china, old paintings; all sorts of valuables." His fingertips drummed on the tabletop. Everything had to be spelled out for Bittner. It was annoying.

"Okay. Once in a while some of these valuables go astray. The Americans can't get enough of them. Hasselblads, Dresden china, original art—Dürers, Holbeins. Anything. You would be amazed, Bittner. And they pay for it in dollars." Sauer glanced at his watch.

New watch, thought Bittner. Sauer was probably dealing with the black market gangs already.

"It is time for you to go and meet Walters and change the money," said Sauer. "I will wait here for you."

Twenty minutes later Bittner parked the truck. He was thinking about the information Sauer had shared with him, but a small encounter he'd had in the lane soon after he'd left the cellar had disturbed him. He had nearly driven into a black Horch sedan, and he'd watched it in his mirror as it turned out of the lane into the next shattered street. There had been two men in the Horch, although he had not been able to see their faces clearly. He had not seen another vehicle in the lane before, and it was rare in these days to see a substantial vehicle like a Horch in the streets. It was the first one he had seen for months.

Bittner climbed down from the truck and walked round the corner into a wide, dusty street. The Americans had managed to get the public transport system working again in the part of the city near the main U.S. Army Headquarters. But except for an occasional tramcar, the traffic was military. He walked past a row of bombed out apartments and came to a small café. Bittner had met Walters there before. It was an arrangement that Sauer had somehow managed to set up. It was a lucrative one for Walters. All Walters had to do was stop into the café for a cup of black market coffee between eight-thirty and eight-forty-five on Tuesdays and Fridays, on his way to work at the U.S. Army Post Office. If Sauer and Bittner wanted to make a transaction they would do it there. Walters would take their Occupation Marks and change them legally at the Post Office. The arrangement was that he would return to the café at ten o'clock with hard U.S. currency—minus a twenty per cent commission for his trouble.

Inside the café Bittner bought a copy of *Die Frankfurter Zeitung* and a cup of coffee from the man behind the counter. The man, who owned the café, took Bittner's money, wiped his hands on a dirty apron and poured stewed coffee into a chipped cup. Bittner took the newspaper and the coffee to a table where he could see everyone who entered the café.

A few minutes after eight-thirty the door opened and a small, bespectacled man walked into the café. He was wearing an army raincoat over his military uniform. Bittner waited while the man bought a cup of coffee. Then he folded the newspaper, left it on the table and walked out into the street. The folded newspaper was fat with Occupation Marks. This was how they did it. Walters would take the *Frankfurter Zeitung* with him when he left the café, and he would bring it back with him when he returned in a little over an hour. If the café proprietor noticed anything he didn't show it. He knew it was wise to pay no attention to such matters.

Walters was an unlikely conduit. He looked like a middle-aged businessman in a tidy army uniform. Bittner had only ever spoken with him once; the week before when Walters had returned with the exchange dollars and suggested he increase his commission. It was a mystery to Bittner how Sauer had contrived to set up the arrangement in the first place. But it had worked for several months.

Out on the street, Bittner had an hour to kill. When he returned to the café he would be a workman dropping in on a coffee break. He walked towards the river, passing a water pump at the corner. Four women were waiting with buckets. A fifth woman was working the pump handle up and down.

The bridges over the River Main were still fractured, although some repair work had begun. Two U.S. Army Bailey bridges provided the only routes to the south shore. A small park of stunted, shattered trees and churned up turf sat next to one of them. Some ducks were paddling on the water by an overhanging willow tree. Bittner liked to go there. It was a small place that told him life would return eventually to the desolated city.

The morning was already warm, the air heavy. The summer weather was holding into early autumn. Bittner looked over his shoulder. Clouds were building in the north-west. It would probably rain later. Perhaps there would be thunder as well. He sat down on the only patch of grass left in the park and watched the brown river. A few kilometres downstream the Main joined with the Rhine, and made its way to the North Sea. He tossed a pebble into the sluggish water. He did not feel comfortable. He was not sure why.

At twenty minutes to ten Bittner got to his feet and dusted off the seat of his trousers. As he turned to walk to the road he heard a plaintive cheeping from the water by the river bank. Two small ducklings swept past, struggling against the current, their little heads darting back and forth in quick, searching movements. There was no sign of the mother. There had been six ducklings when Bittner had first seen them—and the mother. In a city short of food it was probably inevitable.

Bittner was about thirty yards from the café when he heard the sound of an engine speeding up behind him. He knew something was wrong but he stopped himself from turning round. The driver slammed on the brakes when the jeep came abreast of Bittner and the vehicle slewed sideways across the pavement. Bold white markings on the front of the jeep spelled out the words 'Military Police'.

Two white-helmeted policemen jumped out and grabbed Bittner's arms.

The first person Bittner saw in the Guard House at the U.S. military stockade was the man Walters from the Post Office. He was sitting on a bench in a corner of a small waiting room, staring down at his polished shoes, his fingers twining and untwining, fidgeting.

Bittner gave no sign of recognition. He glanced round the room. There were no furnishings except for two benches against opposite walls. The room had a single window, high up, just below the ceiling. It had close metal bars on its outside. The walls of the room were a grimy yellow-white. Here and there a name and a date, or a more defiant obscenity had been scratched into the paintwork.

Walters was taken from the room by two military policemen. Bittner didn't see him again. He was left to sit alone in the waiting room-cell for a long time. Now and then a snatch of music floated through the window from some other part of the building.

You had plenty of money n' nineteen twenty-two,
You let other women make a fool of you . . .

It was after noon before two policemen came for Bittner. Both of them were wearing helmets, both had black armbands with the letters 'MP' in white. Neither of them spoke to him. They took Bittner to a room in another part of the building. Two officers were sitting inside. The MPs left, closing the door behind them.

One of the officers was sitting behind a broad oak desk. The other was sitting on a corner of the desk, one foot on the floor. The officer behind the desk spoke when the door had closed, reading from a sheet of paper in front of him.

"At this time you are charged with illegal dealing in currency. There may be other charges. Have you got anything to say?" He looked up. Bittner shook his head. It was the first time he'd been spoken to since he'd been taken to the Guard House.

The second officer dangled a leg where he sat, swinging it idly back and forth.

"You understand English, Mr. . . . Bittner?"

"Yes sir. A little." He did not know how the officer knew his name.

"Then you had better speak to us. The charge is a serious one. It will be better if you tell us all about it."

Bittner shrugged. "There is nothing to say."

The officer behind the desk considered this. The other man stood up and walked behind Bittner, looking him up and down.

"We have information to the effect that you have been active in black market operations, and that you have been using Corporal Walters to exchange the money you make, for U.S. currency. What do you have to say about that?"

It was a clumsy interrogation, the information too general. But the officer's questions had already told Bittner two things. The first was that they had no real idea what he and Sauer had been doing. The second was that whatever the military police knew, it was information they had received from outside. Bittner wondered where it had come from.

The MPs had picked up Bittner before his second meeting with Walters. He knew he had nothing incriminating on him. Bittner looked the officer in the eye.

"A lot of people are involved in the black market," he said. "But I am not. It is illegal." He shook his head. "This other man you speak about—this Corporal Walters—I have no knowledge of him. I don't know him."

An excruciating pain shot through his body as the officer behind him punched him hard in the kidneys. Bittner gasped, staggered, arched backwards. Another blow followed, this one higher, driving upwards into the side of his spinal column. Bittner fell to one knee, his face screwed in pain, his eyes watering. The room tilted in front of him. He could hear the hazy sound of a radio in the next room.

Snafu. What is the meaning of . . . snafu . . .

Bittner saw silver as the officer who'd hit him slipped a set of knuckledusters into his pocket. The other man came out from behind his desk and helped Bittner to his feet. "Now, now," he said. "We don't want to make things difficult, do we?" He turned to his colleague. "Ah . . . surely we can provide a chair for the prisoner."

Bittner heard a chair scraping on the linoleum floor. He let them lower him into it, aware that the officer who had hit him had moved round behind him again.

"Take it easy for a minute," said the first officer. "Then you can tell us what you've been up to."

Bittner was doubled over, trying to breathe. It hurt too much; his ribs, his kidneys, the muscles in his back. There was a tingling sensation in his right leg, and his arm was numb. He heard a window being pushed open, felt a cool breeze in his hair.

It was minutes before he could speak. "I am a Polish citizen," he said. "You have no right to do this. I want to see a lawyer. I will say nothing until I do."

The next blows came to the muscles above his collarbone, falling on either side of his neck. Bittner tumbled onto the floor. He heard the faint tramp of marching feet somewhere outside. He opened his eyes. The breeze drifted a sheet of paper from the desk onto the floor by his face. One of the officers bent down and snatched the paper away, but not before Bittner saw two words at the beginning of a line. "Kempka's information . . ."

He closed his eyes against the pain. Kempka was the name that Sauer used in their transactions at the U.S. Army Ordnance Headquarters. It was Sauer who had told them.

The officers were not finished with Bittner. It was nearly an hour before two MPs came and helped him from the room. They took him down concrete stairs to a small, airless cell. But Bittner had said nothing more to his interrogators. He lay down on a narrow, hard bunk and pulled a coarse blanket over himself. He stared up at the dirty-white, cobwebbed ceiling, and shivered. Pain flowed through him. Spasms wracked the muscles of his shoulders and back. He began to shake. The man with the knuckleduster had known his business. Somewhere down a long corridor a metal door slammed.

Frankfurt. September 10, 1945—Monday

It was early when Bittner woke up. He lay for a long time on his bunk. A single sunbeam slid imperceptibly down the wall. It would stay in his cell until the sun had risen to a point where the angle was too oblique for the small, barred window to admit. Bittner knew it would leave his cell soon after the light kissed the rim of the toilet bucket in the corner. It was twelve minutes past seven.

Bittner heard boots in the stone-flagged corridor outside his cell, and the rattle of tin plates. A shutter opened, and closed. Then another, and another. There were no voices. The guards didn't speak to the prisoners. Bittner sat up. His muscles ached. There had been no more interviews, no interrogations since Friday. Since Friday he had only seen the cell block guards. There were two of them. Neither one had said a word to him.

The observation shutter opened in his door. Shadowed eyes looked in. Bittner stared back. The shutter closed. He listened to the boots moving away on the other side of the door. The guard had not left breakfast for him.

Five minutes went by. Bittner heard someone approaching, and the bolt drew back in the cell door. A guard, a Corporal, stood in the doorway and beckoned.

"Come on," he said. "You're leaving."

The contents of Bittner's pockets sat on a table upstairs. A U.S. Army Sergeant placed a sheet of printed paper in front of him.

"Sign this," he said.

Bittner tried to read it: ". . . treated in accordance with the laws of . . . has not been subjected to unreasonable duress . . ." They were letting him go. He signed the paper and picked up the items on the table. The Sergeant waited while Bittner threaded the laces through the eye-holes in his boots, and ran the belt through the loops in his trousers. Bittner turned towards the door.

"Wait. We'll see you out," said the Sergeant. He motioned for the Corporal to escort Bittner. "We'll be watching you, Bittner. You don't want to come back in here."

The truck was where Bittner had left it three days before, parked on a piece of wasteland, a bulldozed bomb-site half way between the café and the river. It was hidden from the road, tucked behind a corner of shrapnel-scarred wall. Bittner climbed into the cab, turned the key, pushed the starter button, and held his breath. The engine fired.

When Bittner reached the ruined house near Hanau he put the truck in the tunnel and, out of habit, lowered the tarpaulin. He walked carefully round the side of the house and eased his way down the steps to the cellar. He did not expect to find anything there. The door opened at his touch. He stepped inside, and peered into the gloom. The cellar room was completely wrecked, the cots overturned, blankets scattered, ration boxes strewn across the floor. The ration boxes had been smashed open, and the floor made sticky with melted chocolate, dried fruit and vegetables. The lamp lay shattered on the floor. A smell of paraffin pinched his nostrils.

He inspected the debris, and picked up a tin of beans. One of Sauer's jackets was crumpled in a corner, along with a torn shirt and a pair of trousers. There was no sign of Sauer's shoes. Sauer owned a good pair of boots, which he wore most of the time. But he also had shoes. A man might leave clothing behind, but he would never leave shoes. Shoes were hard to come by in Germany in 1945. Bittner continued to look around the cellar. Apart from the sticky mess on the floor, there was no chocolate anywhere. There were no packets of coffee either. Chocolate and coffee; luxury items. The occupation armies were not short of these things.

Bittner went to another corner of the room, knelt down and began to lever at one of the floor stones with the handle of a spoon. He moved it enough to catch the edge of it with his fingertips, and pulled at it until it came up in his hands. There was a hole beneath the stone, and he reached in and felt around it. It was empty.

Bittner calculated that Sauer had taken nearly one hundred and fifty thousand dollars—the measure of their dealings with the U.S. Army Ordnance, and the exchanges they had made with Walters.

Through the broken cellar window he heard children playing among the ruins. They were playing at soldiers.

Agam Prunt

He was the strangest person I've ever met. I asked him about his name one day.

"It's an unusual name," I said.

"Yes," he said. "It got messed up on the forms. You see, my father had lost some fingers in the war. He had difficulty holding a pencil. English wasn't his first language anyway. Not then. Not until the day he died really."

"The day he died?"

"Yes, his last words were in English."

"What were his last words?"

"*It is better to live in heaven than to rule in hell.*"

"Interesting. That's quite something," I said. "Thoughtful. Shades of Milton."

"Milton?"

I just nodded. Agam wouldn't have understood. He wasn't a student of English literature. It wasn't precise either; not quite what Milton had written.

Agam carried on. "When we checked in at Ellis Island it's what they printed on the form. I guess it's how they interpreted my father's scrawl. Agam instead of Adam. I don't know, I was only four. I couldn't read or write. After that it's what people in America called me. Agam. I think they thought it was a joke."

"I see. Prunt isn't an American name either, is it?"

I have always been fascinated by names. They are clues to the people who own them; almost like nicknames, but more distant, hidden. Often a name would tell of an ancestral occupation—like Butcher, or Baker, or Tanner, or Paynter. Even the name 'Smith' hints at Blacksmith, or Tinsmith—a person who fashions things out of metal.

Sometimes if there was no specific occupation or skill, people were named after a colour that could be to do with hair or their general complexion. Black, Brown, Gray, White, even Green.

Sometimes surnames were place names. Jack London, for example, or Irving Berlin. Abraham Lincoln or Sergeant York. Names could trickle down the generations and apply to people in the present who had no connection to their origins except for a distant genetic link.

Agam said, "My father told me that his people once worked with glass. Some of them had made a living blowing glass, or designing ornamentation for vases, glasses, jugs, mugs, bottles. You know, stylistic, often practical design elements."

"I see. I've never come across the name before in America. What country did you and your father come from? When you came to the States, I mean."

"Germany."

"Germany?"

"Yes. My father said ten generations of our people lived in Germany. Before that they came from Lebanon."

He must have seen the doubt on my face because he said, "That's what he told me. Pliny said Lebanon is where they first made glass. Lebanon and Mesopotamia."

"Pliny?"

"Yes." He didn't tell me who Pliny was, or is. I thought it was an odd name too. I couldn't tell where it came from.

Agam was a bachelor. Not gay, I think; he told me once he'd been married three times. He had very small hands, and on one of them he was missing a finger. It was the middle finger of his left hand. From the puckering of the skin beside the knuckle it didn't look as if it had been surgically removed. I asked him about it that day we spoke about his name. He didn't want to talk about it. Mistaken identity was the only explanation he gave me. A year later when I asked him about it again, we had both had a small glass of wine. I'd forgotten that Agam didn't drink alcohol, and he might have thought I'd given him some kind of juice. It loosened his tongue.

"Someone thought I owed them a debt," he said. "It was painful. No anaesthetic, although they did give me a shot of coke first. They gave me two choices. First choice, an axe or a saw. Second choice, the middle finger or my dick. I chose the axe because it would be quicker. I chose the middle finger because I didn't use it as much as the other thing. It was a small axe. It was quick."

He showed me with his other hand, the one with all the fingers, how they'd done it. He tucked three fingers and his thumb into his palm and laid the middle finger by itself on the table top. "The saw would have been slow and sore," he said.

He didn't say anything more about the other choice. I supposed it was a good thing the people who chopped his finger off hadn't mistaken Agam for someone who'd been messing about with one of their women. He did seem to like women more than men. I think I was the only man he spent much time with, although we didn't see each other often. We only met up once or twice a month, but our friendship, although it was an arm's length one, was consistent over the years.

Despite the mystery of that anomalous adventure, Agam Prunt was what I would call a grey person. By that I mean there was no nuance to him. Nor was there much humour. He seemed to take things literally. Literally. I was never quite sure if he was telling the truth. He had no hair on his head, except for a strange tuft at the back of his skull; the part they call the parietal. He didn't have any eyebrows, and there was no stubble on his chin. I asked him about that too.

"It's a genetic thing," he said. "Something of a curse. I've never had to shave in the morning."

"That's a curse?" I said. "Alopecia of the face. I would think it a blessing."

"Only if you don't have to do it," he said. "It's rituals like shaving that keep people going. They're the things that get you up in the morning. Rituals keep you ticking over; even the ones you don't like."

He saw me shaking my head and pointed, his arm outstretched, index finger levelled at my throat. I put my hand to my chin. I had cut myself shaving that morning and forgotten all about it. I still had a tab of toilet paper stuck there.

"Yes," he said. "You see? You're embarrassed now. But what you don't know is that little cut that won't stop bleeding is what gives you community; makes you the same as your fellow male citizens." He shook his head and there was a sadness to it. "I cannot be part of that community."

"Of course you can," I said. "Who on earth would know?"

"I know, and because of the way the mind works, that is enough."

Agam's knowledge was quite narrow. It seemed to be channeled along strange lines by way of a limited number of subjects he knew a lot about. Other subjects—like geography, or politics, or plants that you thought everyone knew something about—Agam seemed to have no knowledge of at all. To me, this gave him an aura of eccentricity. He wasn't stupid, although because of his strange appearance and his peculiar mind, some people were quick to tag him with that.

He lived in a small grey house at the edge of town. It was an older house, not painted. It was grey because of the siding. The boards on the external walls of the house were made of cedar, and cedar turns grey when it weathers. Agam's house was grey inside too. Grey, except for the things he had hanging on his walls.

There were three paintings hanging in Agam's living room. One of them caught my eye the first time I went to his house. It was a long room and the painting took up most of the wall at the far end of it. The colours were vivid, and the painting showed people at all angles, even upside down. Young people; some black some white. Chaos. Violence. There were painted blood spatters all over it. Agam watched me walk up to take a closer look at it. "The original is in the Museum of Modern Art," he said.

Close to it I could see it was a print; a very good one, and the way it was hung, the light and shadow had made it seem like the real thing. What looked like a real signature was in the bottom corner.

"It has been signed," I said. "Prints don't usually have a real signature on them." I peered closely at the signature. 'Faith Jones'. It was real all right; done with a ballpoint pen—although whether the artist had done it herself I wouldn't have known.

"I'm sorry to say I've never heard of Faith Jones," I said. The imagery and the colours in the artwork were extraordinary. The painting made a statement that was so direct and bright it was like a punch in the stomach.

"You might know her better as Faith Ringgold," Agam said.

That name tweaked a memory. "New York?"

"Harlem. Before she got married her name was Faith Jones. I had the print made up from a photograph."

"But that looks like a real signature," I said.

"It is," said Agam. "I knew her before she got married. I asked her if I could have a high resolution copy printed up, and she agreed to sign it. It's called 'Die'. It's about the race riots in the nineteen-sixties."

It was the only 'real' painting of the three. Real because the other two were, well, colourful, but kitsch.

There were several other things hanging on the wall of Agam's living room. Some of them were reflective. It's difficult to describe what they were exactly. Not wall hangings; more *objets d'art*. Of a sort. Not really my cup of tea. They would catch the light, bounce it around because they would move when a door or a window was opened. Not much, but enough to create shadow and light; indicate motion.

"They're not *objets d'art*," Agam said, as if he was reading my mind. "They are *objets de vertu*."

"I don't know," I said. "What's an *objet de vertu* when it's at home?"

"An *objet de vertu* has provenance, history, substance. It is the product of superior craftsmanship."

I looked closely at the one nearest to me. It was hanging from a broad picture rail by what looked like a piece of fishing line, and turning slowly in the draught from the open door. It was a small, enamelled box, almost heart-shaped. I took it in my hand. "A ladies' powder compact?" I said.

Agam snorted. There was no other word for it. "*Nicht berühren!*" He took it from my hand and let it down gently so that it stayed clear of the wall. "It is a snuff box. Late eighteenth century. You see the enamel? Exquisite! It was painted by Jean-Louis Richter of Geneva. It is worth fifteen thousand dollars. Possibly more. In fact . . ." He tilted his head back and looked up at the ceiling for a moment. "I think it would be closer to twenty, now."

I was surprised that he had spoken so sharply, so instinctively in German. I turned and looked at the snuff box more closely. The enamelled painting showed a galleon, two smaller sailing boats, and a fort on a far shore. In the foreground were two oared skiffs. A young man and woman were on the shore. The young woman was bearing a basket on her head; the young man carrying a sparkled cover of some kind. She was standing still, he was acknowledging her, but taking the sparkled cover to one of the skiffs, which already had a similar piece of weaving draped over its gunwale. The detail was extraordinary, the colours still brilliant after more than two hundred years.

There was another box three feet away, hanging a little bit higher. It was not turning at all, although it was probably subject to the whims of the same draught from the open door. I was not tempted to reach for it after Agam's admonition. Besides, it was less interesting than the enamel snuff box. "Another snuff box?" I said. "Or is this one really a ladies' powder compact?"

"You think it is less interesting than the Richter," Agam said. "I can tell."

"Well, yes. I suppose I do." The box was gold-coloured, with leafy-blue imprinting, and a centre of what looked like two inter-twined musical instruments—a bellows pipe of some kind, and a mandolin.

"It is worth perhaps three times as much as the Richter. It is a Chollet; from Paris in seventeen hundred and fifty-seven. Aymé-Antoine Chollet; thirty-two years before the beginning of the French

Revolution." He looked at me. "Much of it is gold. Do you like gold, my friend?"

That was when I began to discover the secret to Agam Prunt. He was fascinated by gold; by its colour, by its aura, by its worth. Most of all, by its texture; its *touch*. "It is almost sentient," he told me one day. "It's not like a *normal* metal; not like silver, or steel. Of all the metals it is perhaps most like mercury, because it will take on a shape you want—even a texture, like water, like air. It is elemental, and almost infinitely malleable."

One day not long after that, I noticed that his skin seemed to have adopted the colour of gold. It was so palpably unusual that I asked him if he was unwell.

"Couldn't be better," he said. "I made half a million dollars yesterday."

"Congratulations," I said. "Stock market?"

"No. I don't play the stock market. The stock market is for mugs. This was a . . . ah . . . business deal."

"Congratulations," I said again, and waited for him to tell me something about it.

"You're curious," he said, "but you hesitate to ask me about it."

"True," I said. "But financial dealings are private affairs, and if you want to tell me about it, you will."

He nodded; thoughtful for a moment, as if he was making a calculation. "It goes back nearly eighty years," he said. "There were people in Germany at the end of the Second World War who had some . . . ah . . . gold, and they didn't want it to be . . . um . . . confiscated."

Although the things Agam revealed in conversation could appear to be enigmatic, he was normally quite direct in his manner and language. This hesitation was unusual; a verbal stumbling I had not seen before. It piqued my interest. He was quite excited, by which I mean it seemed he wanted to tell me about it. From his manner however it soon became clear there were elements that he would prefer not to share.

"Do you know the best way to hide gold?" Agam's stare was piercing.

I shook my head. "No idea, and I don't expect you're going to tell me it's under the bed, or in a safety deposit box, or anything like that."

Agam grunted. It was half grunt, and half a stilted chuckle that was as much a sneer as anything else.

"Aqua Regia," he said. "Any chemist will tell you that; some grade ten kids can too."

"Never heard of it," I said.

"The King's Water. It's a chemical solution that dissolves gold. It was discovered by Muslim alchemists about twelve hundred years ago. They described it as a mixture of salt and vitriol. Nowadays we make it with a mixture of nitric and hydrochloric acids."

"Dissolves gold? Well, that's not much use is it? I mean if it's dissolved, then it's gone."

Agam shook his head. "You might think so, but it's not the case. The gold still exists. It is suspended in the acid solution. You can reconstitute it as a powder. Basic gold dust. Then you can turn that into gold blocks, or bars, or sheets or whatever form of the metal you want."

"Chemistry was not one of my best subjects," I said.

"It's a simple process," said Agam. "If you understand even a modicum of chemistry there is a basic logic to it." He looked down at his hand; the one with the missing finger. I wondered then if the finger had once had a ring on it; a gold ring. I'd heard that impatient gangsters would chop a finger off to avoid wasting time with soap and water.

"First you want to get rid of any impurities that might be in the Aqua Regia solution," he said. "So, you precipitate them out with Ammonium Chloride. Once you've done that you can add in Sodium Metabisulfite. That precipitates the gold into a powder. The process works much the same way as you make your coffee—with a filter. Then you rinse the powder over and over with water to make sure you get rid of any acid that might still be present."

"Huh," I said. We were nowhere near the purpose of Agam's chemistry lesson, and I knew then he would reveal that to me. I waited.

"The Danes pulled a nice trick with Aqua Regia in nineteen-forty, when the Germans invaded Denmark," Agam said. "There were two Nobel physicists at the Niels Bohr Institute in Copenhagen. They knew the Germans would come to the Institute because Bohr was one of the world's leading scientists, especially in his understanding of quantum theory and atomic structure. The physicists at the institute also knew the Germans would take their Nobel Prize medals if they found them. They were pure gold. So the scientists dissolved the medals in Aqua Regia and put them in a bottle on a shelf with all the other bottles of chemicals in the laboratory. The gold stayed on that shelf until the Germans left in nineteen-forty-five."

I'd heard vaguely of Niels Bohr, but I was getting tired with all the talk. Not only was I not great on chemistry or physics, I was a bit thin on twentieth century history as well. Besides, it was time for me to get back to my apartment. But then Agam rocketed me wide awake.

"My father brought my mother and me to New York when I was four years old," he said. "There were no baggage checks then; certainly not with us. We were just . . . poor immigrants with funny names and funny accents. But along with our meagre possessions my father brought something else with him.

"My father had been a German Army soldier on the Eastern Front; fighting mostly in Byelorussia, and then in Poland. He told me little about it, except that it was a terrible experience: until his last day, that is. He had been ill for a long time, and the house was quiet. We had been tiptoeing about for weeks; not making noise. Then, that day I was told he wanted to speak to me, and my mother took me through to his room and left me with him. I was seventeen.

"He told me his army unit had been driven back by the Russians to a place called Kulmhof, near the village of Chelmno in Poland. One of the Nazis' extermination camps was at Chelmno, and its existence was being erased when my father's army unit came upon it during their long retreat towards Berlin. My father told me that he had killed a Waffen SS guard who was shooting prisoners who had been used to destroy the camp. He said that another soldier in his unit also shot a guard and helped to free the prisoners." Agam looked at me and tears were running down his cheeks. "My father was a good man. He had been conscripted into the Wehrmacht, the regular army. Not SS."

I didn't know what to say. I was afraid to say anything in case it upset him and brought his story to a close.

"My father told me the guard fell and a pack he had on his back made a rattling sound when it hit the ground. My father picked it up. It was full of gold teeth." Agam gave me the strangest look. "The teeth were in our baggage when we passed through Ellis Island in New York ten years later."

"Oh my goodness," I said. "Teeth?"

Agam nodded. "Gold teeth. One hundred and sixty-two of them. Altogether they weighed just under thirty pounds. My father had divided them up among the three of us; my mother, myself and him. Ten or twelve pounds each for him and my mother, and a smaller amount to go in with my belongings. Of course I didn't know we were carrying several pounds of gold. The teeth were high-value ore; an average of close to twenty carats. It wasn't like it is nowadays. If you get a gold tooth now it will be about ten carat: half the purity it was then."

There had been a change in Agam's demeanour while he was talking. A few minutes before, when he was speaking of his father, tears had been coursing down his face. Now he was dispassionate; a mathematician crunching numbers.

"Do you know how many ounces of gold go into a tooth?"

I shook my head. "My crowns are porcelain," I said. "They were expensive enough as it is."

"About three, if it's good quality," he said, "and those teeth were good quality."

I noticed his use of the past tense. He had said the teeth *were* good quality.

He pulled a gold watch from his pocket and studied it for a moment. "It's four-fifty," he said. "In ten minutes we can listen to the stock market report if you want. It will give us today's gold price. But yesterday it was one thousand six hundred and nineteen American dollars and ninety-nine cents per Troy ounce. That's for pure gold, and the teeth my father acquired were not pure—but they were close to it. To get a safe evaluation you could knock ten per cent off. So, let's call it fourteen hundred and sixty dollars an ounce."

My brain was churning; sixteen ounces in one pound times fourteen hundred and sixty dollars, times thirty pounds.

Agam was reading my thoughts, or else they were printed in capital letters on my face.

"There are a little more than fourteen and a half troy ounces in a standard pound; a standard avoirdupois pound, that is. The total value would therefore be about six hundred and thirty-five thousand dollars," he said.

"My father was afraid to try and sell the gold. As a commodity, gold was treated with great suspicion for years after the war, because it was known that high ranking Nazis had managed to secrete gold from the country, or hide it away inside Germany."

I nodded, as if I knew what he was talking about. The thought crossed my mind that Agam was spinning me a yarn; that his father had actually been one of the guards at that camp. I flinched at what that might have meant. But the tears would have been difficult for Agam to construct. I said before that he was something of a grey person; that his personality was flat, rather emotionless. In fact, early in our relationship I had considered that he might be something of a sociopath, possibly even psychopathic. I hesitate to admit it was a quality I found intriguing in him, but it was true. Now, I was waiting to hear about the '*were*' part of the story; about what had happened to the teeth.

Agam smiled. "That's the part where I ultimately lost the middle finger of my left hand. By the time we had lived in New York for about ten years my father had become friendly with a neighbour, an

Irish man by the name of McCarthy. Mr. McCarthy's sister was married to an Italian gentleman, a Mr. Cravatta. Lucio Cravatta." Agam paused, looking at me, as if to see if I indicated some recognition. But I had never heard the name before.

"They lived in the next street to us in the Bowery district," Agam said. "Eldridge Street. I remember that Mr. Cravatta always wore a neat, but nondescript, bow tie.

"In the course of time Mr. Cravatta introduced my father to a Mr. Herdman. This Mr. Herdman was a jeweller of sorts. My father told me he used to design jewellery, and cast his own metals to make rings, pendants; things like that. Trinkets my father called them. Mr. Herdman was also a goldsmith, however, and he had done some . . . ah . . . work for Mr. Cravatta." Agam cleared his throat, turning his head as he did, as if he found it difficult to swallow the phlegm he'd coughed up.

"To cut a long story short, Mr. Herdman produced eleven sheets of gold for my father. One of the gold sheets was to be a . . . ah . . . commission on the transaction. Payable to Mr. Cravatta for making the introduction." Agam sighed. In a different circumstance I might have taken it as a sigh of regret.

"A single sheet of pure gold, one millimetre thick, and measuring eight and a half by eleven inches—your standard size for foolscap paper—weighs about forty-one ounces. But we're not talking about Troy ounces anymore; we're calculating that refined weight in avoirdupois. Instead of fourteen point five ounces to the pound, we've now got sixteen ounces in every pound. Which calculates out to a difference of roughly two thousand four hundred and thirty dollars per sheet."

My brain was becoming foggy, but I was just about able to understand that Mr. Cravatta had been short-changed by Agam's father to the tune of approximately twenty-four thousand, three hundred dollars.

"You're saying that the commission was paid with a sheet of gold that was calculated in Troy ounces, and not in avoirdupois," I said.

My attempts at these mental gymnastics were giving me a headache. It occurred to me that there might have been another discrepancy as well. That would have been if the associates had been given a sheet that was not quite as pure as the sheets Agam's father had taken. Goodness knows how much of a difference that would have made to the value of the 'commission'.

"Yes," said Agam. "That is what I am saying. That, and the ten per cent commission was calculated on a smaller amount than my father and Mr. Herdman had declared. It took Mr. Cravatta a while to work that out, and of course my father was dead by the time Mr. Cravatta and Mr. McCarthy came to talk to me. I was eighteen by then, and I told them I knew nothing about it; that I didn't have any gold. Nonetheless I acknowledged the fact my father might have made a mistake. They were not pleasant people, and so as recompense I offered them the Richter snuff box, which had also been acquired by my father. But they didn't want it; they wanted the gold." He coughed.

"In the end they saw that they could kill me, and that would make a mess, and would not get them their money. But they wanted some measure of satisfaction; they did not want to simply go away and forget about it. That's when they offered me the choice I told you about before." There was a thin smile on his face. "It was unpleasant."

"The purity of the gold," I said. "It was the same with all the sheets?"

The smile thickened slightly. "You're a perceptive one," he said. "Remind me to count my fingers after I shake hands with you in the future. It turned out that Mr. Herdman was indeed something of an alchemist. For a little bit extra for himself, he made the commission sheet from the inferior gold he extracted from the teeth. The commission sheet was only about half the value of the other sheets."

"But you said the gold teeth were high value; about twenty carat gold."

"Yes, well, not all of them were. Twenty carats was an average. Pure gold is twenty-four carats. Some of the . . . ah . . . original owners, had had teeth extracted and replaced with pure gold before they were arrested by the Nazis. My researches told me this was not an uncommon precaution against future destitution. Others had not been able to do the same thing—or not to the same degree of purification. Mr. Herdman, in his processes, had separated things out; the inferior from the superior. From what my father told me before he died, I understood that was an agreement he and Mr. Herdman had come to. Mr. Herdman's Irish and Italian associates had apparently become aware of that . . . ah . . . irregularity as well."

"I don't suppose Mr. Herdman is still with us," I said.

"Good heavens no," Agam said. "This all happened many years ago. Besides, Mr. Herdman's associates were extremely unhappy with him. They believed he had played a significant part in what they saw as an act of dishonesty. Mr. Herdman had met with an accident shortly before the two gentlemen came to see me."

It occurred to me that Agam must have made a calculation at that time about the value of his middle finger, and probably about the pain that would be associated with its removal.

"When you come to a new country, a new culture," Agam said, "it doesn't matter how young or old you are, you learn very quickly that you rise or fall depending on the degree of wit you have. We had nothing of value when we came here—except for a bag of teeth my father had acquired. But by the time I was eighteen I had lived in New York for fourteen of the most formative years of my life. Even though I was not as worldly as my two visitors, I knew that the Irish and Italian gentlemen would not simply take what they thought they were owed—perhaps another sheet of the gold, or even two. I knew they would take it all if I was to reveal where it was. My good fortune, and Mr. Herdman's misfortune, lay in the fact that they considered Mr. Herdman to have had as significant a role in the whole proceeding as my father. They could do nothing to my father because he was dead. But because I was my father's son—and a possible beneficiary of his duplicity—they needed to extract some satisfaction from me as well. But not my life, since they saw me as peripheral to their original agreement. It therefore came down to a finger, a threat, and a warning."

"A threat?" I said.

"The threat lay in the choice they gave me. My finger or that other thing."

I looked down. I didn't want him to spell it out to me in the crude manner he had before.

"And the warning?"

"Yes," he said. "They made that quite clear. If it were to reach their ears that a number of sheets of pure gold had appeared anywhere on the eastern seaboard of the United States, they would assume they had come from me." Agam smiled. "I have kept my eye on these two men since I was eighteen years old. Neither of them had sons. One of them had a daughter. I think of her as 'the Irish daughter'. She inherited her father's money and became a philanthropist. She invested his ill-gotten wealth in arts centres and artists, in the symphony, and particularly in operatic works. She is a bit like me, with my fondness for creative works, I suppose."

He paused. "Mr. McCarthy somehow fell from the Manhattan Bridge twenty years ago. The Italian gentleman died yesterday. He was ninety-three years old. Yesterday is the day I made half a million dollars."

Agam got to his feet. He smiled, tapped his forehead in a little salute and turned, as if to leave. "You will excuse me," he said. "I have things to do."

He departed without saying anything more about Aqua Regia, or about the Irish Daughter; leaving me with only my own suppositions, right or wrong.

Danang

I had been in Danang for four days before the night Lanh turned up on his motor scooter. "Hop on the back," he said. "I'll give you a tour of the city." He produced a crash helmet for me to wear.

It was hot and I was tired. I'd intended to stay in my air-conditioned room at the Sea Phoenix Hotel, maybe take a dip in the rooftop pool after I'd rested. The juggler barman up there would provide entertainment. He always did. He never had many customers. It was worth the entry charge to watch him throw half a dozen bottles in the air and catch them. It was just the price of a beer. There was hardly anyone staying at the hotel.

Lanh's arrival changed my plans. "You can sit in a room or swim in a pool, or drink beer anywhere," he said. "You can't see Danang every day, not when you live half a world away." Lanh was the only person I'd met who could speak English. The only Vietnamese word I knew was *Bia*. The juggler barman had taught it to me. It was the most obvious word for beer.

Lanh was my interpreter. He was a small, intense man with coal-black hair; much younger than I was. I'd been sent to Danang to teach courses in hotel operations.

"Keep your knees in," Lanh said when I climbed on the scooter behind him. "You don't want to lose your kneecaps." Then we were off, gathering speed down Ho Xuan Huong Street.

It was a long time since I'd sat on the back of a motor scooter. I remembered to lean into the corners with Lanh, but I wasn't sure if I should hold him round his waist or not. In the end I put my hands behind me, where they could grasp a small rail at the back of the pillion seat. Then we were at a roundabout and in among hundreds of other motor-scooters, and the milky-warm air was thick with fumes.

Lanh half-turned his head. "Kneecaps! Keep in." I tightened my thighs on the side of his thighs. There wasn't much room on the back of the scooter.

I shouted above the crackling noise of engines. "What are the rules at roundabouts? Who's got the right of way?"

Lanh turned to look at me. I'd rather he'd have kept his eyes on the traffic as it zipped and dashed chaotically around us. He had a big grin on his face. "No rules," he said. He turned back to see where he was going, and leaned hard over and we shot off down a side street. A minute later we were speeding across a bridge over a river.

He turned his head again. He seemed to feel it was polite to turn round and look at me when he was speaking.

"Han River. It runs through the middle of Da Nang, divides the city in two."

On the other side of the river we were in the old part of Danang. Low buildings crammed together. Narrow streets. Lanh took me to what looked like a semi-derelict building. It was higher than the buildings around it, but not much, maybe three floors high. There were windows on the middle floor, but none on the ground floor. No doors either, just an opening in the wall. He parked the scooter and pocketed the key. As we headed for the opening, I asked him why he didn't lock the scooter.

"No need," he said. "No one will steal it."

I was surprised to see a food vendor's operation inside. Half a dozen rickety tables and chairs open to the breezes. There was a big old Gaz cooking stove against one wall. I tried to remember where I'd seen a cooker like that before. France perhaps; it looked old enough to be a left-over from the time Vietnam was called French Indochina.

A woman standing behind a small service counter looked up when we came in. Lanh said something to her, and they exchanged a few words. I noticed she had only one arm.

"If we're going to eat something here," I said, "I have to find a bank to get some money."

"No need," Lanh said again. "Not eat here. We go to get *Bia*."

"Money," I said. "I still need to get some."

"They do money change," he said, "but no need." Lanh took me up four steps to a small landing and pressed a button on the wall beside a stainless steel door.

I wasn't keen on using my credit card in that place, and it didn't look as if they would take travellers cheques. To tell the truth I was beginning to feel a bit nervous. I'd only known Lanh for a few days, and we'd had a falling out over what I thought was his habit of abbreviating my comments in translation during one of the hotel operations sessions. I had given a detailed explanation of protocol and procedure for room service—for when hotel staff had to enter a room when it was occupied by a guest. Lanh had encapsulated it into three sentences. I told him he couldn't possibly have explained everything I'd said.

"Yes, I explained," Lanh had said. "It was simpler the way I put it. They understood."

The stainless steel door slid open and we were staring into a big industrial service elevator. I'd never seen one so shiny before. Lanh stepped inside. "Come on," he said. He must have sensed my reluctance. He pushed a button beside a small plaque that read, 'Schindler'.

The room service session the day before had hit a bigger difficulty soon after the first one. There had been three young men and three young women on the hotel's room service staff. At one point I had asked them who made up the beds. They all put up their hands.

"And who cleans the toilets?" I asked. The young men laughed, and made faces. The young women looked away. One of them said, "We do."

I asked why it was only the women who cleaned the toilets in the rooms. Lanh translated all of it. Back and forth, English to Vietnamese, and Vietnamese to English.

"It is women's work," said one of the young men, and the other two laughed again.

"Why?" I said.

Lanh's translation of my one-word question was the opposite of abbreviated. He spoke for nearly two minutes. That made me just as cross as the previous incident. This time he'd put words into my mouth instead of taking them out.

After the session I'd given him a bit of a telling off. I told him that I was here to give these sessions because I was an expert in hotel management and operations. He might be a professional translator, I said, but he wasn't qualified to do anything more than translate what I said to the staff. He hadn't liked it. All this came back to me as we went up in the elevator.

The elevator stopped and the door opened to the night. The top floor was a kind of deck area, open to the sky. Street sounds floated up from below; motor-cycle engines, a car horn, a woman's voice calling to someone. In an apartment building across the way someone was playing a trumpet.

The roof was flat, and ringed with a low brush fence topped by a foot-wide wooden ledge, like a shelf where you could put food or drinks. The air was sweet. Jasmine, bougainvillea and hibiscus blossomed in big pots. Searchlight beams swept back and forth across the river, picking out puffs of speckled cloud. We could see the river bridges lit in different colours, different artistic styles.

A few round tables and tall wooden stools were scattered around. It looked as if the roof was a bar of sorts—but where were the customers for such an exotic setting? Then a tall, older man stepped from the shadows and greeted Lanh with open arms. He wore a black shirt and loose black pants. One side of his face looked as if it had been bashed in with a sledgehammer. He spoke out of the side of his mouth in short, staccato bursts. I don't know what he said to Lanh because it was all Vietnamese, but he took Lahn's handshake in both of his hands with a great warmth, and kissed him lightly on the top of his head.

They conversed for two or three minutes, Lanh turning once or twice to indicate me. He didn't introduce me.

"Would you like *Bia*?" said Lanh.

"Yes," I said, "but I've only got a couple of American dollars with me."

"No need," Lahn said. "He won't take American dollars *dù sao*."

"*Dù sao*," I said. "What does that mean?"

"It means he will never take American dollars." Lanh looked at me as if to say that part of the conversation was over. "I told him you are Canadian." He sighed. "There is no *Bia hoi* here. No draught beer. You can have Heineken or the local beer—Tiger or Larue."

"Tiger," I said. A big raindrop landed on my head.

"What do they do during the monsoon?" I said when Lanh came back. He handed me a bottle of Tiger.

"They get wet," Lanh said. "I don't come here then."

"What kind of *Bia* have you got?" I said. He was holding a red bottle in his hand.

"Not *Bia*," said Lanh. "Doctor Thanh. It is a herbal drink. Healthy. Better than *Bia*."

All through this, the tall man who had greeted Lanh stayed in the shadow behind what must have been the bar. The counter was shaded by a low awning. It was difficult for me to make things out in the darkness. There were no lights up there except for the searchlight beams, and some reflection from the nearest bridge. I took a sip from the bottle of Tiger beer. There were no glasses. The humidity was making me sweat. Lanh hadn't touched his Doctor Thanh.

Lanh made small talk. The man behind the bar counter stayed where he was. Silent. The lights played across the sky. There was a peal of thunder, and some raindrops.

"We should go," I said.

"Why?" said Lanh.

"Big day tomorrow. I've got to speak about the front desk operation. I need to do some preparation before I turn in."

Lanh said, "He is my father. The woman downstairs is my mother. You don't need to be afraid." He put his hand on my arm and gave it a small squeeze. "They were hurt by bombs when I was a child. Now I have good work and I was able to buy this building for them. When I have more money I will get more of it repaired." He smiled. "It gives them something to live for."

It was the way he said it as much as anything else. I knew it was true and I knew I had misjudged him. I felt badly for it and I didn't know what to do.

"I'm sorry," I said.

"It made life hard for them. They were younger than I am now. They could not get work. They had to wait, and hope that I would grow into a person who could help." Lanh picked up his Doctor Thanh and drank from the bottle. "They have no family except for me."

"They must be angry. Bitter," I said.

Lanh looked at me and shook his head. "No. It is not their way. Not the way of people here. It is *now* that is important. *This* day. And this day they have hope."

Cardozo

Cardozo gazed out of the window, across an expanse of tarmac and grass to the hills beyond. He had a dream-like look on his face. A clock ticked loudly on the wall. The Station Manager waited patiently for Cardozo's reply.

"Again, Mister Cardozo, please tell me where we can find the reference point for this airfield." The Station Manager glanced at his wristwatch. The clock ticked.

"Why do you wear two watches, sir?" said Cardozo. He had the title of Second Assistant, Air Operations. He was in training for promotion to First Assistant, Air Operations. Cardozo believed the best way to learn was to ask questions. His questions were not always relevant to the task at hand, and he didn't always pay attention to the answers he got.

The station manager looked at the watch on his right wrist, the one that showed Greenwich Mean Time. He looked at the watch on his left wrist to check the local time. A flight was due to touch down in twenty-eight minutes.

"Don't answer a question with a question, Mr. Cardozo. Please answer the question I asked you."

Cardozo continued to gaze out of the window. A minute went by. "It is there," he said.

"Where?" said the Station Manager.

"Out there." Cardozo pointed at the window.

The Station Manager dropped the thick text he was holding in his hand. It landed flat on his desk and made a loud bang.

Cardozo jumped.

"It is indeed out there Mr. Cardozo, but I want you to tell me precisely where, out there."

Cardozo had turned to face his manager.

"It is also in here, Mr. Cardozo. In this textbook." The Station Manager jabbed at the book with his finger. "If you had read it as I directed you to, you would have been able to answer my question." He sighed. "The Airfield Reference Point—the A.R.P.—is the centre point of an airport. It is located at the geometric centre of all the usable runways. In technical terms it is computed as a weighted average of the end of runway coordinates. In today's world it is a set of coordinates we obtain by what we know as a Global Positioning System."

Cardozo stared at him. The crash of the book landing on the desk had given him a fright. His first thought was that he had been shot. The Station Manager was an impatient man, easily irritated, quick to anger. Cardozo would not have been surprised if he had shot him with the pistol he kept in his desk drawer. The Station Manager was staring back at him, his eyes bulging as they did when he was annoyed. *Exophthalmia* it was called. Cardozo knew this from the optometry studies he was undertaking. His father, who knew his son well, had insisted that he should have a 'fall-back' in case a career in aviation didn't work out. It was a guiding principle.

"Global Positioning System," repeated Cardozo.

"GPS," said the Station Manager.

"Yes, GPS."

The Station Manager glanced at the watch on his left wrist. The incoming flight would land in fourteen minutes. "We will continue this later," he said. "I shall see you in here at fifteen-thirty hours." He turned, picked up the duty folder, placed his airline cap on his head, and walked out into the empty, marble-floored Arrivals Hall.

Covid-Nineteen

"You can look, but you cannot touch, and you cannot speak. They cannot know that you are there."

"What will happen?"

"If you touch, or speak?"

"Yes."

"You will be gone."

We were above the earth, descending fast. There was no sensation of speed or of movement.

"I am already gone," I said. "There is a marker on my grave; a granite stone. My name is on it, and a poem."

"That will remain. It is the afterlife that will cease to exist." His name was Thiurmann. He was in charge. I didn't know what he was in charge of. Perhaps only me. I thought I would find out in time. I couldn't tell where he was from. He spoke with no discernible accent.

The earth was coming up quickly, but I could tell that our rate of descent was slowing. Yet there was no sensation of deceleration.

"What is the purpose of this?" I said.

Thiurmann stepped away from the controls. It wasn't that he had no personality, or character, or that he spoke without undue expression; in every aspect he was like a normal being. But clearly he was not. It would take me time to work out the kind of being he actually was. In the meantime the craft could fly itself. Or he could operate it by transmitting his thoughts and directions.

"You must understand," he said, "that this is what happens to everyone who dies in one of the less advanced societies such as the one you have come from. Because you have had the power of thought, of study, of consideration and of . . . possibilities, you were given the opportunity in your world to explore for yourself what might lie beyond your sentient life. But you didn't take the opportunity. Like most people you put it off and put it off. Death was something that happened to others, not to you."

I held my hand up. "I'm not one of those people who put it off and put it off until it could not be put off any longer. I did try, but it was beyond my capability to come to a resolution."

"You could have taken up one of the world's religions," said Thiurmann. "There are answers in each of them for many, many people. Buddhism, Christianity, Islam, Zoroastrianism, Hinduism, Taoism, Sikhism . . . Bahá'í perhaps, since it teaches its adherents to value all religions."

"I could have," I said, "but I didn't think I would find an answer in a book that someone had written. Not even in a book that tribes, whole peoples, had written."

"Books are signposts," said Thiurmann. "They point the way to a destination. You simply have to want to go to that place; that end. It's not complicated." He was shaking his head. "Books and signposts. They're not *dictats*. It's up to people what they take from books."

I could see green fields now, and brown hills. We were getting close. We passed over a great city to more countryside, and grey stone houses here and there. The features went by so quickly it was impossible to recognise any of them as places I had known. From what Thiurmann had said a short while before, I knew he was taking me to see people. But where, and who, and to what purpose? I could see people now as we came closer to the ground. People like ants. Thousands of them. Millions. In some places there were so many of them they blotted the colour from the land, so that it was black.

"Won't they see us?" I said.

"No," said Thiurmann. "They cannot." He gave no explanation.

We were moving slowly now down a city street. There were tramcars moving along tracks. Pedestrians were walking on one side of the street looking in shop windows. I could see faces, and it seemed as if I would recognise someone at any moment, but I didn't. Not on that street. We passed over a bridge, and came across a young man wheeling a push cart with a child in it and I knew the child was me. The man was my father. He stopped at the bottom of a stone staircase, picked up the cart and the child and climbed the steps. Thiurmann stopped us there and I could look into my father's face. It was full of pain.

"Remember what I said. You cannot, must not speak, and you cannot touch. Everything you do, you must do with your mind." Thiurmann was watching me closely. "You can do anything with your mind," he said. "You can touch them with a thought, perhaps a sensation. You will see."

We moved on and we were again in countryside, above a grassy field among rolling hills. A misty grey and white dog was herding sheep, bringing them in a small group to a boy. The boy was myself, four or five years older than the child in the push cart. I could look into the dog's eyes. One eye was brown, the other was blue. The sheep stopped, six of them, and the dog lay down at the feet of the boy. The look on the boy's face revealed that he was happy. He patted the dog on the head and the dog wagged its tail.

A woman came out of a house nearby. She was wearing a light summer dress. It was yellow with blue designs on it of sea shells and sea horses. She called to the boy in the field, and he turned and the dog stood up. The dog and the boy walked across the field to the house. The woman gave the boy a kiss and took him into the house. The dog lay down on the doorstep. The woman was my mother.

"Can I hear sounds? Voices? Birdsong?" I said.

"Traffic?" Thiurmann smiled. "Explosions. Shouting and swearing at a football match. Running water. Waves crashing on a beach?"

"All those things. The precious and the tragic."

"You were able to hear those things when you were alive," said Thiurmann. "Did you?"

I didn't answer him. Instead I said "Scents and smells? Like Milton's *tedded kine*. Flowering privet after a summer rain; woodsmoke from a beach fire?"

"Ah! The stench of a sewage spill. The odour of cow dung. Don't forget the sweat of fear. You could smell all those things when you were alive. Did you?"

"Yes," I said. "All those things. They are life; they tell us we are alive." I looked at him. "I may have failed in many things, but I at least knew the senses, all of them."

Thiurmann smiled. "Perhaps you're not ready yet."

"Perhaps not, but I want to see what you have to show me before I decide." I surprised myself with that. I had no idea what I was stepping in to.

"Very well," said Thiurmann, and in a second we were thousands of feet above the ground, above clouds, to where we could see the curvature of the earth. Again, there was no sensation of movement. No gravitational force at all.

"I would like to see where you come from," I said.

"You have seen where I come from," said Thiurmann. "It is where we came from today. I cannot take you there again. Not just yet. Not until we are finished here. There are things you must still see."

"What is its name?" I said. "I forget."

Thiurmann stared at me. He turned around, all the way. Three hundred and sixty degrees; as if to see if someone else was with us. He smiled again. I was beginning to find his smile irritating. "Covid-Nineteen," he said.

"It's an unusual name for a place," I said. "Does it have an atmosphere? Does the sun shine? Do flowers grow?"

"Of course," said Thiurmann.

"How would I know that?"

"If you believe it, it is true."

"What if I don't *quite* believe it," I said. "Almost perhaps, but not quite."

"Then you must trust me."

We were stationary. The earth was no longer receding below us. I looked around, trying to get a sense of what was propelling us across what seemed to be a sky I had known my whole life. I could make out the curve of the earth, blue water, grey and brown land, some green here and there, a sweep of white cloud, whorls and fantails. Then, a speck, far below, climbing quickly towards us.

"What is that?" I said.

"It is one of their advanced aircraft. Rocket powered. Probably military."

"Does it mean us harm?"

"It might mean us harm, but it cannot cause us harm." In an instant the aircraft seemed to stop, and stay in the same place. I realised that it had only appeared to stop relative to where we were, since the earth continued to turn below us.

"We can let it keep station with us," Thiurmann said. "We select a distance and it cannot get closer, no matter how fast it can fly."

That way we went around the earth for a short while. Africa passed beneath us, and the expanse of the Indian Ocean. Australia went by, with the triangle of Tasmania hanging upside down below it, and we were over the Pacific. When we neared Mexico the speck, the rocket plane, began to fall away. Thiurmann slowed everything down. "There is no need for us to hurry," he said.

There was silence for what seemed a long time.

"Taste," said Thiurmann.

"Yes, yes," I said.

It was irritating, condescending. Thiurmann had answers for everything. If I told him I liked the taste of ice cream, I knew he would counter with something unpleasant.

"All right," he said. "Feel then. Feelings."

Reluctantly I said, "Love; that feeling of nerves you get when you're thirteen years old and you ask someone out for the very first time, and they say yes."

"Huh," he said. "They say 'no'. It happens all the time."

I was expecting that. "Orgasm then," I said. "Once you know it's going to happen there's nothing you can do about it. Nothing you can do to stop it."

We began to descend very quickly towards the ground. I was

waiting for Thiurmann to come up with his usual, negative riposte, but he didn't say anything.

"Orgasm," I said again. We were getting closer to the ground. We passed over high mountains, and then blue water, until we came to land. I felt a sense of anticipation, but it seemed as if Thiurmann was slowing our progress. He was staring straight ahead, a fixed expression on his face.

Then I recognised the village where I had lived; where I had loved, had children, and a brown dog and a grey cat; where I had built a house to live in; where I had been roused from sleep at a springtime sunrise by the hammering of a woodpecker, and heard the songs of blackbirds and bluebirds, smelled the scent of flowering madrona, felt the touch of a breeze through an open window, and been rocketed wide awake when a child jumped onto my bed.

"You've never had one, have you?" I said.

Thiurmann wouldn't look at me.

"It's life," I said. "Magic. It's being alive. Giving life."

Thiurmann brought us gently to a place where I could touch the earth, and I stepped away from him. There were no clouds in the sky. I smelled salt from the nearby sea. The sun was shining.

The Stones of Gleann Meurain

For the late Bob Bissett of Glen Lyon,
who made violins and brogues, and told me about the Stones.

"It's time for him to come." She stared through the window at the glen. The grass was green and bright, the hummocks spiked with sharp reeds and the coarse rushes the sheep wouldn't eat.

"It's early yet," said her husband. "The snow's not been gone for long. There will be more growth before he comes." He gazed down at the child. "Are you all right, child? You can wait a little longer, can you not?"

The child looked up at him, then at its mother. It answered the question with one of its own. "How long has it been since he was here last?"

"September," said the woman. She was watching a stag which had breasted the stony hill opposite the cottage. "It was the last week in September." The stag stood still, scenting the wind, watching the croft. She could see the breath coming from it.

"He'll do the thatching this year," the father said. "It's due. The roof leaked in the winter."

"You said that last year," the woman said, "and the year before that."

"It's every seven years he does it."

"I'm cold," said the child, "I want to go into the sunshine."

"You'll have to wait until he comes," said the woman. "We can't go out until he comes." She sighed; the waiting was more difficult the closer it was to his coming. The stag moved cautiously down the hill towards the croft. It was a Knobber, a young one, no more than two or three years old. She heard a sound and listened. It came again;

the high mewing cry of an eagle. It was behind the house. It was a strange call for such a powerful bird.

The sun was sinking behind the hill, the long, wide shadow of the ridge reaching out for the house.

"He'll not be coming today," the woman said. "He'll come in the morning so he can get home before dark." She sighed again. "How long is it we've been here now?"

"I don't know," said her husband. "It has been a long time."

The narrow front window afforded only a limited view down the glen, but they knew of his coming long before he came into their sight. The first sound came from a flight of grouse that scared up near the place where two streams join. A deer could have frightened the birds. None of them spoke; they listened, until they heard the sucking of his boots in the deep, wet peat to the south of the croft.

Sound carried a long way in the stillness of the glen. It had been a long time since the place had echoed with the cries of children, or the lowing of cows; longer still since drovers had cursed and caroused cattle down the track to the market at Crieff.

"He sounds tired," the woman said. She could hear his breathing in the quiet air.

"Ssshh." They listened again.

"Older," she whispered. Her hearing was better than theirs. "His lungs are not as good as they used to be."

"Maybe he's been inside all winter like us," the child said. "Maybe he needs sunshine too, to bring him back to life."

The mother thought kind thoughts of her child at that, but she didn't move to touch it. Instead she listened harder. "He's close now. Just another few minutes."

They felt excitement, each of them in their own way. It was a special thing, this visit. The highland man only came to them twice each year. The woman thought he might do the thatching this time. It was always a good thing when the old roof came off and the dark inside of the croft filled with light. When he did that the hill wind blew away the dust and cobwebs, and made everything fresh; at least for the summer, until the winter dark came down again. The croft never seemed to recover well from the first winter after a thatching though; it was always a long wait until the next year.

"I can't hear him," said the child, and it began to cry softly to itself. "It's not him at all, it's only a tramper. He's not coming after all."

"There, there." The child's father had a pang of doubt, but he kept it to himself. "He'll come. If it's not him now he'll come tomorrow, or the day after, or the day after that. But he'll come. He always comes."

The child sobbed quietly. "You've never told me what would happen if he doesn't come, father. What will happen if he doesn't come?"

The father shivered. "It's not the time to talk about that. We can talk about it later."

"The child will need to be told," the woman said.

"*Wheesht*," her husband said. "I can hear him now; he's close by."

They held their breath and listened. They could hear his boots turning down the grasses, and they caught the sigh of the turf as it sprang back with his passing.

"He's not heavy-laden," the woman said. "He's not carrying much with him. I can't hear the clinking of tools. He won't be planning to do the thatching this time."

A shadow passed across the window, and the door opened, squeaking on its hinges. Light flooded onto the stone floor, and then a shadow fell as the highland man stood and surveyed the inside of the croft, blocking out the sun. He was a big man, kilted as he always was, his boots wet on the flagstones. His breathing was heavy. He was tired from his journey.

He spoke to them as he always did, in a tongue they didn't know themselves, but which they were able to understand through its cadences.

"You'll have thought that I wasn't coming." He took off his pack and set it on the floor at his feet. "The weather's made me a bit late this year. There was snow down below until last week. But there's no need for you to be worried about me. I'll be coming here until I can't walk anymore."

It's not so much for you that we're worried, thought the woman, it's for ourselves because we'd be lost if you didn't come.

"When the day comes that I cannot hike up here there will be another one to do it for us," the highland man said. He reached into his pack and pulled out a small fiddle and held it by its neck. "Unless…" he muttered to himself.

He set the fiddle down on the dusty table and the bow by its side, and reached into the pack again, and brought out a wrapping of oatcakes and a small bottle of the *uisge beatha*, the whisky.

"I'll play you a tune when I've had some sustenance." He patted the fiddle. "It's a new fiddle too. I've made it myself. It plays a good tune all right." He took a bite from one of the oatcakes, and spoke again although his mouth was full. "It's not been a good winter down in the glens. There's been snow. A lot of sheep got caught in the drifts. McNaughton lost six ewes and a dozen tups, and the Englishman Taylor lost nearly half his flock." He raised the whisky to his mouth.

It seemed to the woman that he drank from it for a long time. Her husband tasted it as if he'd had a drink of it himself; felt the warmth of it coursing down his own throat.

"They're not used to the suddenness of the weather, the English," the highland man said. "Not used to the blizzards. But then this is no place for southern people." He wiped the back of his hand across his mouth.

It will be dark inside for another year thought the child. Mother is right; he will not do the thatching this time. Oh, how I want to see the light again. The father savoured the afterthought of the whisky and was content for the moment.

The visitor finished the oatcakes, and took another draught from the bottle, and put the cork in it and placed it on the table. "I'll not have any more of that now. It's a long way home and I smelled snow on the wind. We could always have a late snow. You can never be sure."

He reached for the fiddle and brought it up to his chin, and placed the bow gently on the strings. He drew the bow back and the notes came together in a piece of beauty and softness, and the sound of it floated out the door and into the wind and mingled in the glen with the long grasses and the heather, and blew down and down to the place where the two streams meet.

To the child it was the most beautiful sound it had ever heard. It must be a magic violin, it thought, and if the highland man had made it himself then he must be the cleverest craftsman in all of Scotland. If I could only listen to such music every day then I would be happy for ever.

It was a fine thing this; every time the highland man played his music it seemed to the child as if it was hearing it for the very first time. And yet he played the fiddle for them each time he came, two times in every year.

"That was for the glen," the man whispered when he had finished, and the child saw that his eyes were moist.

I wish you would play us another one before you leave, thought the woman. Not so much for me, more for the child. She felt an unaccustomed tenderness for her husband. Play it for him too; for all the years we've passed together.

The highland man lifted the bow again. It was a lighter tune than before, a chattering melody, like the sound of water rushing over stones. The child's mood changed with the music and it felt light and happy, as if sunbeams were dancing on its skin.

The highland man put down the fiddle. He patted the child on the head and let his breath come out between his teeth. "It keeps me right, to come up here. I don't know what I'd do if I'd not got that. It'd be an awful sacrifice."

The child felt the highland man's warm hand, and the kindness in his voice. The father waited; he wanted to go out into the sunshine, but he was the head of the family and he would wait. The others would go first.

The woman heard the highland man's bones creak as he rose. She caught a strain in his voice, and felt the cold touch of apprehension. You're an old man now right enough she thought. You're as old as we've been in this place and that's a long time. I cannot believe there will be a day when we'll not see you again. You've been coming here for as long as I know. There is responsibility in that, and trust. You cannot abandon us. You have to pass on your knowledge to someone else.

"Aye," he sighed, "I'll not be doing the thatching this time. The grasses are not right for it; they're too brittle yet. The cold has bled the warmth from them. I'll make you a promise though. When I come back in September I'll bring my tools, and if all is well I'll do the thatching then."

He took the bottle from the table and put it in his pack, and swept the crumbs from the oatcakes onto the floor with the side of his hand. He picked up the fiddle and the bow and wedged them into the pack, and turned down the flap, and fastened it. The door was open and he walked to it and looked out at the hillside, up at the sky and sniffed the wind. There was a faint scent on it of wildflowers. Cranesbill, and Kingcup. It was a soft wind, perhaps a springtime wind. He caught a suggestion of the fragrance of Sweetgale.

"You'll be fine," he said. "I don't think it's going to snow after all. I think we've had the most of it now." He picked up his pack and took it and set it down on the wet turf just outside the croft. Then he went back inside and bent down and picked up the child and took it to the doorway and placed it gently on the wide, flat threshold stone, so that if the door blew closed the child would be in the open air. He patted it lightly on the head, and turned back for the woman.

She was heavier than the child, and he held one of his hands under her and supported her head with the other. He placed her beside the child, carefully, on its left side. Lastly he picked up the man and took him out and put him to the right of the child, so that there was no way in or out of the croft except to pass around them. As an afterthought he patted the man's head.

"You're a man," he said softly. "You'll not get so many kind words, but you're just as precious as any of them that was born here."

He hoisted his pack on his shoulder and started off down the glen. It would be dark by the time he got home. The man and the woman and the child watched his back recede down the hill towards the place where the two streams met. They listened for the last of his footfalls, but the wind had moved around to the north, and they lost the sound of him long before the sight of him merged with the colour of the hills.

The child felt the sun on its face and the breath of the wind, and was happy. The wind brought with it half-forgotten scents of sorrel and bog myrtle, and the rich, damp peaty smell of the northern hills. There were new shoots on the rushes, and the grass would green more every day.

The father could still feel the warmth of the highland man's touch on the side of his head, and the tang of the whisky, and was sated with the simple pleasure of it. The mother knew that it was more complicated than that. She understood that the highland man represented the changing of the seasons, the circuits of the sun and the moon, the measure of the ages. He came to the shieling each spring and placed the ancient stones in the sunlight, and returned before the first frosts of autumn to put them back inside. She knew that every seven years he came and cut the marram grasses in front of the cottage, and bound them loosely together to renew the thatch, so that the child and the father and the mother would be dry.

She knew that as long as the highland man did those things, the stones would protect the glens, and keep them fertile, and safe.

The Stones: Handing on the Task

"Do you want to go up to the shieling in the morning, Coinneach?" Donnachadh asked.

"I think so." The highland man turned a lump of peat in the fire. A puff of thick, sweet smoke blew into the room. "Yes, I think so. It's time."

"It's a long way for an old man. It is rough ground now; not like it was when the track was more often trod."

The highland man nodded and his eyes were distant in the flames from the fire. He wrapped his hand round his glass to warm it before he took a sip of the *uisge beatha*—the whisky.

"They know more than you and me up there, Donnachadh," he said. "They know about change; they feel it in the air. They know where it will take us. The woman especially."

Donnachadh Anderson considered this for a while, and the fire smoked and the clock ticked on the wall beside the highland man's violin, which hung there like a maturing capercailzie. He reached for the bottle on the table and poured whisky into his glass.

The highland man leaned forward, and bent down and loosened the laces of his brogues. "I've been at this too long already. My time's nearly done. Soon it will be up to you, Donnachadh."

The first day of April was a fine day. The highland man and Donnachadh were up at the head of the River Lyon by the time the morning sun cleared the round back of Meall Ghaordaigh behind them. Frost lay on the ground like fine-milled oatmeal, sparkling in the light, crunching under their feet.

The two men turned the corner into Gleann Meurain and followed the stream, keeping up the hillside to stay clear of the wetland.

It was hard going, and neither of them spoke. After an hour they crossed the burn and passed into a smaller glen, and climbed for another mile or so over broken, tussocky ground, past old peat hags.

The highland man's stride made adjustments automatically for the unevenness of the ground. He did not slow down. Donnachadh was younger by thirty years, but he had difficulty keeping to the old man's pace. They passed the place where the two streams meet, and the highland man stopped.

"They'll not be expecting us," he said. "We must be respectful, and speak to them and explain what it is we're doing. They will want us to be clear about it."

Donnachadh said nothing because he needed the break to catch his breath. There was a lot of work to be done before they would pass this way on the journey home. They would be well tired by then.

They came to the top of the rise and the shieling was huddled against the side of the glen, near a mountain burn. The stones would be standing inside the door, waiting. Donnachadh had not come this way for several years. He stopped to let the power of the place wash over him, and in that moment he fancied he saw the shadows of the children who had brought cattle to these summer grazings in times long past. The lush, green places where the grass had been cropped and fertilised spoke to him of the sheep and cattle, and the people who had brought them here down the centuries.

The highland man waited, knowing that Donnachadh's thoughts would be like the thoughts that came to him whenever he visited this place. Then the two men made their way across the floor of the glen to the ancient croft.

The highland man spoke softly to the stones. When he'd finished explaining what they had come to do, the two men took the shovels they'd brought and began to dig a circle in the turf around a small, grassy mound in front of the croft. It was nearly an hour before the highland man put his shovel down. He stretched out the muscles in his back for a long minute before he reached into his pack and pulled out a bottle of milk, a packet of oatmeal, a pat of butter wrapped in grease paper, and four eggs. He poured the milk and the oatmeal and the butter into a bowl, and broke the eggs on top of it, and stirred the mixture with the blade of his knife. While he was doing that Donnachadh scoured about behind the shieling for sticks and heather roots, and made a heap of them at the centre of the mound. When that was done, he pulled dried grasses from the ground and stuffed them under the twigs.

When the highland man had finished stirring the mixture in the bowl into a custard, he put the bowl on the ground. He looked over at Donnachadh, and held his eyes. He wanted to be sure that the younger man understood. Then he got to his feet and walked to the door of the croft, and knelt on the threshold stone in front of the man and the woman and the child. Donnachadh stayed where he was by the mound. This was something for the old man to do by himself.

The highland man wanted to speak to the child because he knew the child would understand the least about what was to happen. But he looked at the woman first because she understood the most of them, and she would explain it later to the child in her own words, so that it would not be afraid.

"You'll know what we're about to do now," he began, "and I want to be sure that the wee one is not frightened. Your husband too, I don't think he can see things in the same way you do. But I want all of you to know that there will be nothing to fear from the fire, and that Donnachadh and me will take care of you. What we're going to do is just to be sure that you're protected, and that we are too."

The child thought, but can we not have a new thatch before you go away again? Just one more from you; a good, strong one to take us through the winters until somebody comes to look after us again?

The highland man scratched his head for it was not in his plans to come back again to this place. He looked at the child and nodded.

"September," he said. "September will be a good time for the thatching. The grasses will be stronger then."

The child remembered that he had said the same thing before, and he'd come and thatched the roof, and so it trusted that a new thatch would be cut and laid before the next winter.

The highland man stood up and they could hear his bones creak as he rose. You're an old man now right enough thought the woman, not for the first time; older than my imagining, and that's saying a lot. I cannot believe there will be a day when we'll not see you again. She looked at Donnachadh standing by the mound with the sticks heaped up on it. He has a strong face she thought, weathered with the winds, and his eyes are keen. They won't miss much. Maybe he'll grow to have the wisdom of the highland man. Perhaps he will be all right for us if the old man doesn't come back. And she knew that if he'd been chosen by the highland man she could have trust in it.

The highland man reached down and picked up the child in his hands and carried it to the shallow pit they'd dug around the mound. Then he went back for the woman and took her out to be beside the child, and set her down gently on the child's left side. He went back again to the threshold, and picked up the man and spoke to him quietly as he carried him to his family.

"You've said nothing since we got here," he said, "but you will be thinking." He stopped, and cradled the man in his arms. "She's got the sight that one," and he was talking about wisdom. "And you have the strength. You should never forget that together you have a power that nothing can touch. Nothing." He walked on a few paces. "It's for the bairn and all the young ones to come that we have to do this." He placed the man carefully beside the child, on its right side.

Then he took a flat rock the size of a supper plate and placed at the centre of the sticks on the mound, and on it he put oatmeal he'd fashioned into cakes the night before. When that was done that he took a match and struck it, and held it to the dry grass under the sticks, and the wood blazed up bright, and the sky grew dark with clouds that had gathered over the glen. He nodded to Donnachadh, and Donnachadh picked up the bowl from the ground and handed it to him. The highland man poured a little of the mixture onto the turf at the feet of the stones, and offered the bowl in turn to each of them. The woman first, then the man; lastly the child. When he had finished the offering he handed the bowl to Donnachadh, and Donnachadh drank from it and passed it back. The highland man held the bowl to his lips and drank from it himself.

The fire was bright so that shadows danced across the hillside. The old man reached down for the woman and drew her into his arms. He held her tightly and jumped through the flames to the other side of the mound.

'Latha nan seachd sian.' The old man's voice came from the back of his throat, welling from deep inside him.

The woman felt the vibrations of it, because the sound of it was as old as there had ever been people in that place. He is calling on the day of the seven elements thought the woman. He is calling Air, Water, Earth, Fire, Light, Darkness and Spirit, and she was afraid for her child.

The highland man put the woman down in the shallow trench they had dug, so that she was placed on the far side of the flames from her family. Then he walked around the fire to the man and picked him up, and leapt through the flames and took him to the woman.

'Oidche nan seachd sian'

The man felt the power of an ancient voice, and knew that the highland man was calling upon the night of the seven elements to follow the day, and he was afraid for his wife and for their child.

Then the highland man picked up the child and cradled it in his great hands, and jumped through the fire one more time.

'Deireadh nan seachd sian orm'

And the child heard the words which called for the dissolution of the seven elements, and it was afraid because it thought that the world would come to an end. The highland man placed the child in the trench between its father and its mother.

"Now young Donnachadh," said the old highland man, and his voice was different than it had been when he'd spoken in the Gaelic. "You'll do the same thing as me, and take the woman and the man and the bairn through the fire, and when you've done that you'll place a charm on each of them to keep them through the difficult times to come. You are the future, and they need to know they will be safe with you."

Donnachadh took the child first, and wet his hand with his tongue and rubbed it on the child's head and carried it through the fire, stepping through the flames in an unhurried way, and the fire didn't burn him.

'*Cuirim an seum air do chom, chum do thearmaid*'

And the child heard him and knew it would be protected and safe.

Donnachadh carried the man into the flames and out the other side and said,

'*Dionar tu a thaobh do chuil, is tu an eala chiuin s' a bhar.*
Cha teid gu brath ort ailis.'

The man took in Donnachadh's words, and knew from them that he would be brave and would never know disgrace, and that was the most important thing to him, and he was comforted by the certainty of it.

Last of all Donnachadh took the woman and ran his strong hands over her so that she would feel the life in them. He walked with her through the smoke and fire and said,

'*Rach ruaig rath an alachd, car nan coig cuart s' nach falbh am fear sin uat.*'

And the woman understood that she and her family would not be barren, and that her people would always be faithful to her.

The highland man knew that Donnachadh's words would comfort the child and the man and the woman; that they would have confidence in him. He took a strong, forked stick and lifted the flat stone with the oatcakes from the fire.

They are not ordinary oatcakes thought the woman. There are two of them and each one has bumps on it like little paps, and there are seven of them on each cake.

The highland man handed one of the oatcakes to Donnachadh and took the other for himself. He stared into the heart of the fire and broke off one of the knobs from the oatcake, and threw it back, over his shoulder.

"This I send to thee, Eagle; to watch over my shieling."

He broke off another of the lumps and threw it behind him as well, saying, "This is for thee, Wolf, to preserve my livestock."

And again with a third, "This is for thee, Fox, to be clever and keep you my seed."

With the fourth he said, "I send this to you, North Wind; preserve my pastures."

With the fifth he said, "This is for you, Rain, to keep all my rivers, and the fish in them."

He broke off the sixth lump and tossed it behind him, not taking his eyes from the fire. "This I send to you, Earth, to preserve my customs and my language."

The last one he threw into the middle of the flames and said, "This is to you, Fire; you must keep my people."

After each incantation, Donnachadh had done the same, and when he spoke after the highland man he was aware of a strange depth and timbre in his own voice.

When the highland man and Donnachadh had finished they ate the oatcakes. "This will keep our people safe until the stones have done what they will do," said the highland man.

He stood up, and took the woman and carried her to the doorway of the croft and put her down on its threshold. He did the same with the others, and set them so the child was in the middle, and the man and the woman on either side in the places they were supposed to be.

Before they left, the old highland man stood in front of the stones and spoke to them. A sudden wind came up as his voice rose, and plucked at his clothing, and tossed his hair about his face, as if the power of the mountains was in him.

'Gun robh agaibh fad nan seachd bliadhna, tu neart gaoithe, agus talmhainn agam air.'

The stones stood in the doorway and the light from the fire flickered over them, and the flames crackled as the sticks split with the heat and spat out moisture.

The fire died away with the footsteps of the highland man and Donnachadh, and it was quiet again in the glen, except for the wind, which fell until it was barely enough to bend the grasses. The two men stopped at the ridge line and looked back at the shieling, and turned and walked on for a little while.

"How long have the stones been here?" said Donnachadh when they came to the place where the two streams meet.

"They've been here for a long, long time." The highland man spat into the confluence of the waters and made a wish. He knew it wasn't necessary; it was just for insurance. "The stones contain the life of the glens. The power of all the elements lies within them." He looked at Donnachadh. "All we've done is to confirm that; release it. Renew it."

Then the old man reached out and took Donnachadh by the shoulder and said, "My bones need to know that you understand it in the way that I do."

Donnachadh felt an electricity through him, a flow of strength from the highland man to himself, and it seemed to him as if he rose up from the ground and looked down on that place from somewhere in the sky. He saw the rocks melt and form again and the ages rush past, until at last he heard the cries of people and the lowing of cattle in the glen. He saw the cycles of eternity, and he understood then that the highland man was the changing of the seasons, that he represented the circuits of the sun and the planets, the measures of night and day; and with it came an immense confirmation that what he was involved with now was an essential thing—an essential thing.

Donnachadh knew then that he would come to the shieling each spring and take the ancient stones into the sunlight, and that he would return again before the first frosts of autumn each year, and take the stones into the shelter. He knew too that every seven years he would cut the marram grasses by the cottage, and bind them loosely together and renew the thatch, so that the child and the father and the mother would be dry and warm. Donnachadh knew that this was his responsibility now; that as long as he did these things the stones would keep the glens abundant and safe.

The Stones:
The End, and the Beginning

"How long have the stones been there?" Donnachadh asked again, on the way down from the place where the two streams meet. "I didn't understand the whole of it; the answer you gave me up on the hill." He paused, slowing his pace. "The *why* of it; I understand that. But *how* did it come about?"

The highland man slowed his pace as well. "The stones have been there a long, long time," he said. "They were put there in seventeen-eighty-one, when the last of our people were cleared from that place. It was the year the land was taken up by a man of title from the south. He put the people out to make way for sheep." The highland man spat into the marshy bottom at the side of the track and made another wish. He knew it wasn't necessary, but you can never have too many wishes in order to make sure.

"The stones contain the life of the glens. They hold the power of the elements. All we've done, is unlock that." He marched on down the glen, and he felt an anger moving inside him. "It's something we could have done a while before we did. Should have, even."

"Aye," said Donnachadh, because the power of the stones was no longer beyond his imagining. "It surely is a good thing we do it now, is it not?"

The highland man stopped. The sweep of Gleann Meurain lay in front of him, reaching down to the burn at its foot, the burn that becomes the River Lyon; the burn that would in time produce the waters that became the loch at the head of Glen Lyon. But it was still an empty place, Gleann Meurain, with no grazing land, just the tracks of deer; its only sounds the whispering of the winds in the hill grasses and the calls of birds.

"Yes," he said.

All winter long the rain and the snow fell, and the wind blew in its turn. In the spring that followed a late snow interfered with the lambing, and the damp gave the cattle afflictions of the hooves and congestions of the lungs. Tapeworm and roundworm thrived in the unusual conditions, and the livestock became thin and weak. As the summer wore on the old man pointed out the signs to Donnachadh, and the two men took precautions wherever they could to protect their own stock, and the crops they had planted for food. Late summer winds knocked the crops down but the heather bloomed and turned the hills to colour, as the leaves turned brown and fell from the trees. The air was hard in October when they set out again to climb the hills, and follow the deer trails up into Gleann Meurain.

They kept to the hillside until they had climbed past the place where the two streams meet, because the rains had saturated the lower ground and it had become uncommonly marshy. They topped the last rise and looked down on the shieling.

Donnachadh had been up to the shieling by himself some months before in the spring to put the stones out on the threshold to watch over the glens. It had been the first time for longer than he could remember that the highland man had not gone up to the *tigh* himself. But now there was a thatching to be done, and it had to be done the right way. He turned to Donnachadh. "I wanted to feel it in my bones again that you understand it the way I do." He said it just as he'd said it before, but he wasn't quite finished. "And I wanted to stand with you and the family up there one last time."

He reached out and took Donnachadh by the shoulders as he had before. And Donnachadh felt the electricity in him again, the flow of strength from the highland man to himself, and it seemed to him that he rose up and looked down on that place from somewhere above it, as he had the year before. He saw the rocks melt and form, and floodwater and ice over the land, and the ages passing until he heard the cries of children and the lowing of the cattle. He understood once more that what he could see was a vision of the cycles of eternity, the rotation and the preservation of life. And he knew for the first time that this was an *agreement*; a binding transaction with an entity he did not wholly comprehend.

The highland man took his hand from Donnachadh's shoulder. "It is to make sure; why I'm here. Not just that," he said, in case Donnachadh thought he had a doubt. "It is to help with the thatching this last time. So you know the way of doing it at this *Tigh*."

They cut reeds behind the shieling and tied them in bundles, and the stones were there, on the threshold, watching. Coinneach and Donnachadh set the bundles of reeds on the roof and bound them with twine to hold them against the winds, but not so tightly that the twine would cut into the stems and bleed the life from them. When the thatch was on the roof, the old man looked up at the sky.

"We've not got much time," he said, for he could feel the strength leaving him. The younger man could do the heavier work while he went to gather moss from the rocks. He collected mosses and worked them with his hands, and stuffed them into the crevices in the walls of the shieling to keep out the prying winds. While he was at this, Donnachadh cut thick sods with his shovel and placed them in squares on top of the thatch so they would give it some protection from the rains.

The dark was coming on them by the time they finished. The old man knelt on the damp ground beside the stones, and the setting sun cast his shadow on the wall of the croft.

"It will be seven years until one of us comes to put on a new thatch, and it won't be me; it will be Donnachadh. My time is done now. I've helped you keep the glens for as long as I've been able to. We've put moss in the walls to keep out the wind, and we've put turf on the thatch to keep it until Donnachadh comes to check on it in the spring."

He spat on his hands, and rubbed them together. Then he touched each of the stones in turn on its head. "You ken the whole of it now."

On his knees still, he picked up the child and moved it inside the door so it was under the new thatch. He reached for the woman and put her down beside the child, and then he lifted the man and put him beside the two of them, to make three. "It's a good number, three," he said. "A timeless number. Together you are the past, the present and the future. Everything there is, there was, and will be."

The highland man stood up, and walked to where he'd put his pack, and took out his fiddle and bow. He hoisted the pack on his shoulder, and nodded to Donnachadh.

The two men set off down the glen and neither of them looked back. When they came to the brow of the hill where they would be lost to the sight of the stones the highland man stopped and raised the fiddle to his chin and turned. He began to play, and as he did the strains of the past and the future rose up the hillside, and hung there on the wind, and came round again with its currents. The child at the shieling felt comfort in the music, and knew that it need not be afraid.

The highland man is as old as the stones. He is the spirit of the glens, and their custodian. He is in the earth and in the rocks. His essence flies with the winds, and lies in the rains and in the snows. At night, in winter, you will find him in the fires of the shielings. He will always be there.

Acknowledgements and Notes

Acknowledgements

My thanks and appreciation to my wife Marilyn Bowering for her help, encouragement, and her patience in reading these stories, making suggestions, and for her advice with the edits.

My thanks too, to Barry Smith of Dowie's Mill at Cramond, Scotland, and sometimes of the hamlet of Bastard in the Ariège, France, for his encouragement and perceptive comments.

'Danang' could not have been written without the seminal experiences I shared in Viet Nam with Nam Tran Ky of Da Nang. I also wish to recognise the support I received from Phung Trong Hieu of Ho Chi Minh City, and Phuong Dao Thi Ngoc of Da Nang.

I am grateful to Michael Ondaatje, who kindly took the time to check 'Queenie' for any egregious errors in my depictions of Ceylon/Sri Lanka. Any faults or inaccuracies that remain in the tale are entirely mine.

My thanks are due to Robert Bringhurst taking the trouble to read the manuscript, and for his helpful linguistic and stylistic suggestions.

On a wild winter night in front of a peat fire, the late Bob Bissett of Cashlie in Glen Lyon recounted the outlines of an age-old story of ritual and renewal that I have fictionalised in the three parts of 'The Stones of Gleann Meurain'. Bob was part of that ritual for much of his life. I will always be grateful to him for bringing this aspect of the ancient past of my native land so viscerally alive, and for putting me in touch with it. Bob Bissett's papers are lodged at Castle Menzies at Weem, near Aberfeldy, Perthshire, Scotland.

My thanks to Sharron Gunn for her assistance with matters concerning my use of the Gaelic in 'The Stones: Handing on the Task'.

I would be remiss if I did not recognise Margaret and Stan, my late mother and father, for the extraordinary experiences early in my life of West Africa, and later, my stepfather Stewart Wilson for similarly important learnings. For while this book is a work of fiction, some of it inevitably relies on people and events that are only a shift away in time.

Notes

The Title Story: 'Transactions with the Fallen'

Few people alive today know what it was like in Germany in the years immediately after the Second World War; the daily challenges civilians faced in finding shelter and food, in trying to scrape a living, in simply staying alive, and the lawlessness. Much of Europe was in a state of chaos for years, such was the damage to cities, industry, and the essential infrastructure of civilised life, social and material. There was little transport. Road and rail networks were broken. There were no medicines, and not much in the way of health care. There were few shops for people to buy food, no work for people to earn money, no industry to supply jobs.

There was never enough food in the cities. What little there was, was strictly rationed, unless you were fortunate enough to live in the countryside near a farm. Germany's cities were in ruins; great piles of dirt, bricks and wood with tracks bulldozed through them. There was an odour to it as well, of damp and mould; of death in the ruins. Many former soldiers lived in holes in the ground, even two and three years after the war had ended. Germany was fertile ground for banditry and gangsterism after the war.

'Transactions with the Fallen' gives a tiny glimpse into that world of vanquished and victor, chaos and disorder.

The first snatch of song lyrics overheard by Bittner during his interrogation in the story 'Transactions with the Fallen' comes from the song, 'Why Can't You Do Right?', written by Kansas Joe McCoy in 1936.

The lyrics from the song 'Snafu', overheard a few minutes later by

Bittner, were written by Harold Adamson for the 1944 film *Four Jills in a Jeep*.

THE STONES OF GLEANN MEURAIN

As I noted in the acknowledgements, Bob Bissett told me many years ago about the Stones, their antiquity, and their importance. Bob was, in essence, the keeper of the Stones.

The Gaelic incantations in the second of the stories—'The Stones: Handing on the Task'—are taken in part from the Carmina Gadelica, Volumes I and II.

The quotation that concludes this book comes from a very old introduction to 'The Voice of Thunder' in Volume III of the Carmina Gadelica. It speaks to the time of the Clearances, times of great suffering for Scotland's Gaels, when people were driven from their land and their homes, and their culture was torn apart. It is intended to reflect as well my respect for the peoples of Canada's First Nations, and to recognise their anguish and agonies at the hands of an invasive culture that was too ignorant to understand the fundamental importance, the essential nature, of what it was to lose by its actions and decrees.

> *The reciter said: The old people had runes which they sang to the spirits dwelling in the sea and in the mountain, in the wind and in the whirlwind, in the lightning and in the thunder, in the sun and in the moon and in the stars of heaven . . . I remember well the ways of the old people. Then came . . . eviction, and burning, and emigration, and the people were scattered and sundered . . . and the old ways disappeared with the old people. Oh, they disappeared, and nothing so good is come in their stead.*

Printed in the USA
CPSIA information can be obtained
at www.ICGtesting.com
JSHW082359230724
66692JS00002B/80